For a few moments I sat dazed and motionless in the basket that had wedged itself between two trees and was now swaying threateningly in the wind.

"Hey, are you all right?" an apprehensive voice called from Earth.

"Fine. Where are you?"

"Here. Right here."

I tried peeking through the needled branches but couldn't see anyone. "Step farther into the clearing. I can't find you!"

"How about now?"

"That's better!" I said as I spotted a pair of eager, brown eyes above a light sprinkle of freckles. "Do you live here?"

She nodded. Her auburn hair whipped gracefully to-and-fro in the wind. She was small and slender, probably younger than I. She might have been really pretty, but it was kind of hard to tell as she appeared to be dressed more like a marine than a female.

Dear Readers:

Thank you for your unflagging interest in First Love From Silhouette. Your many helpful letters have shown us that you have appreciated growing and stretching with us, and that you demand more from your reading than happy endings and conventional love stories. In the months to come we will make sure that our stories go on providing the variety you have come to expect from us. We think you will enjoy our unusual plot twists and unpredictable characters who will surprise and delight you without straying too far from the concerns that are very much part of all our daily lives.

We hope you will continue to share with us your ideas about how to keep our books your very First Loves. We depend on you to keep us on our toes!

Nancy Jackson
Senior Editor
FIRST LOVE FROM SILHOUETTE

UP IN
THE AIR
Carrie Lewis

First Love from Silhouette

Published by Silhouette Books New York

America's Publisher of Contemporary Romance

SILHOUETTE BOOKS
300 E. 42nd St., New York, N.Y. 10017

Copyright © 1987 by Carrie Lewis

ISBN: 0-373-06227-3

First Silhouette Books printing March 1987

America's Publisher of Contemporary Romance

Printed in the U.S.A.

RL 5.3, IL age 11 and up

First Love from Silhouette by Carrie Lewis

CARRIE LEWIS comes from a family of pilots, as First Love readers may have guessed from *Head in the Clouds*. Before becoming a full-time writer she held down a variety of jobs. Among them she lists guidance counselor, secretary, waitress, deli manager and sales clerk. She now lives in the Arizona desert with her husband and their two small children.

Chapter One

The rock ridge was weathered to a steely smoothness. Its sides protruded skyward like giant marble pillars, and its top, oddly flat, was tinted orange in the midmorning sun. It was an awesome sight. More beautiful than I'd thought it could be. Perhaps it was worth my dangerous journey to scale it. The winds were developing so unpredictably that it might have easily become my last.

But I didn't much care.

To most people, this mass of copper-colored slate was just another stiff ridge bordering the colossal ravines of the Grand Canyon. But to a guy in a hot air balloon, it was a stone giant waiting to eat anything stupid enough to come close. I was covering a lot of country at thirty miles per hour and, I don't know, maybe it was the challenge of it, or perhaps, like I said earlier, I just didn't care.

Making a snap judgment, I decided to fly the towering cliffs ahead. I pulled the trigger on the blast valve and headed toward the heavens.

Some balloonists would call it irresponsible, or more specifically, moronic. My fuel was low. The wind was crazy. My landing was guaranteed to imitate a yo-yo, if not a falling egg.

I floated above the crimson giant with only five hundred feet to spare. Six mule deer bolted from beneath a piñon tree like a burst of fireworks. A violent wind shear scooped me higher, and the gondola was pushed outward, giving me a stomach-wrenching view of the forest cascading down the opposite mountainside. I buckled limply to the bottom of the basket, my adrenaline redlined.

Suddenly I realized I wasn't ready to die.

I focused on the instruments. Eight thousand feet above the ground, and I was on my last tank of propane. I shut down the burners. I'd blasted quite a bit to climb the ridge to avoid smacking into it. Now the prolonged silence was reminiscent of a soft padded cloud. Soon the pyrometer reading began to sink, and the altimeter continued to drop.

I tried to relax. After all, I would live at least until it was time to land. The earth was coming at me rapidly, and I began scanning the valley for a suitable clearing in my path.

There wasn't any.

That was another reason hot air balloonists without brain damage don't fly over dense, rugged forests. Balloons are without steering and must go where the wind pushes them. The biggest talent a pilot can have is the ability to read and locate desired air currents. Upon landing, he must get the balloon low enough—and in exact timing with his speed—to drop to a small patch of dirt without any permanent rearrangement of his body parts.

I gazed outward against the sun. There was no dirt here. Only pine trees shoved against more pine trees. I tried to envision a landing on one of the pointed saplings. Either I'd crash through its branches and be pineconed to death or the top would bend back like a sling and hurl me across the Grand Canyon.

Not very encouraging. Finally I spotted a bald patch of ground. It was in my path but still a good distance away. The tough decision now was whether to make the series of blasts needed to reach it or to save my fuel for the landing. A tree crash would probably rip the envelope beyond repair, while a landing without fuel would only make my legs shorter.

I blasted. As the balloon journeyed closer, I noticed a large log cabin situated at the edge of the clearing, nearly lost in a thicket of trees. Shortly after, I ran out of reserve fuel.

With the wind's help, I'd almost made it. The balloon was low and level, and I knew even if I broke a leg or two, I'd probably still live. I braced myself as the gondola began a rough succession of collisions with the treetops. I was a Ping-Pong ball trapped in a wicker casket. After one particularly hard crash, I opened the deflation port to its maximum, and the roller coaster ride was over.

I sat motionless a few seconds, feeling myself for missing parts. The basket was wedged between two trees and swayed threateningly in the wind. Most of the envelope had miraculously landed in the clearing and was now blown tightly against the trunks of the bordering trees.

"Hey, there! Are you all right?" an apprehensive voice sounded from Earth.

"How does the balloon look from there?" I asked, feeling my way cautiously to the opposite side of the basket.

"I don't know exactly. I think it popped. It's flat anyway. Are you all right?"

"Fine. Everything's still attached. Where are you?"

"Here. Right here."

I tried peeking through the needled branches that had pinned me in, but I couldn't see anyone. "Step farther into the clearing! I can't find you!" I yelled.

"How about now?"

"That's better." I spotted a pair of eager, green eyes above a light sprinkle of freckles. "Do you live here?" I asked.

She nodded. She was younger than I, small and slender. Her auburn hair whipped gracefully to and fro in the wind, and I would've considered her pretty except she was dressed more like a marine than a female. Interesting was a good word for her. Interesting and tomboy cute.

A youngster in green corduroy overalls and no shirt clung tightly to her leg.

"My name is Edon, Ed for short. And this is my little sister, Melissa. My other sister, Cristy, was here, but she ran inside to comb her hair when she saw you coming."

"Be quiet, potato head!" A hushed snarl sounded from the shadows. A blond girl several years older than Edon stepped into view. "Hi. My name is Cristy," she announced.

"Hi." I folded one of the rips in my shirt closed.

Cristy was a heartbreaker. A full-fledged porcelain dream girl beamed to Earth from Venus.

"That's some balloon you have," Cristy said.

"Thanks."

"It's flat." Edon pointed her finger.

"Are you injured?" Cristy asked.

"I already asked him that."

"Can I ride in it?" Melissa looked at Cristy.

"It's flat," Edon repeated.

"I've always wondered what it would be like to go up in a balloon," Cristy said.

"What a dreamer! You get dizzy stepping into the bathtub!"

"Have you been a pilot long?"

"What do you think, Cristy? He landed in the trees."

"Does that man have a bathroom in there?" Melissa asked.

"Blowing that up must've taken a long time." Cristy looked impressed.

"I don't believe her." Edon rolled her eyes.

"It must demand lots and lots of courage to go up in a balloon. Does it?"

Most females talk, but I was beginning to notice that this girl, Cristy, purred. She shaded her blue eyes and tilted her head slightly as she smiled up at me.

"Do you think I could go up with you?" she asked.

"Flat. No air. Do you understand?" Edon reminded Cristy.

"Sure." I leaned over the padded trim to see her better. There might've been a few wisps of copper in her hair, but I couldn't be sure. Maybe her eyes had a tint of turquoise in them, too.... The wicker gondola began to tilt with my weight, and, with the suddenness of a heart attack, I instantly realized my mistake.

One of the branches supporting the basket cracked ominously, and I began to sink. Another branch snapped, and the next thing I knew, the ground was rushing toward my face.

"But I could feed him and brush his hair, and I promise to keep him clean," the tiny voice whined.

"That's not the point, Melissa. He's not a stray dog who needs a home. I'm sure he has a family somewhere that's very worried about him," a woman answered.

"It's kind of strange, Mom. Most balloonists have chase crews that follow them to their landing place."

"I know, Ed. But how could anyone follow him over the canyon and forest? The wind was strong yesterday. Maybe he was blown out of contact with his friends."

It was difficult for me to tell if the voices I was hearing were real or a part of a dream. My mind was lost in an overpowering fog. Even when I heard sounds and wanted to wake up, I couldn't seem to concentrate long enough to get my eyes open. It was pitiful. I'd fade in and out, in and out, as though I had a battery on the blink.

"Then his friends should've reported him missing."

"I know dear. Maybe they will."

"His eyes sure are black."

"That's what happens when you break your nose."

"Do you think he'll remember anything next time?"

I had no idea who this poor sucker was, but I sure felt sorry for him. Black eyes, broken nose, no friends—what a mess.

"But what if he doesn't have a home?" It was the tiny voice again. "He could share my room and live here. I know! I'll give him Baby Wet to sleep with."

Baby Wet?

"Yeah, Mom, he could bunk with us."

"I hardly think so."

"Please, Mommy. He looks so awful. He needs someone to love him."

"She's got a point there."

"Please. Baby Wet wants him to stay. She misses Wayne a lot."

"Wayne?"

"A lot."

Suddenly it was very quiet.

"Ohhh, Melissa...honey..." The woman's voice broke, and a few seconds later I was sure I heard crying. Footsteps followed, and the weeping sounds faded.

I forced my eyes open.

"You shouldn't have said that, Melissa," a girl with auburn-colored hair said softly. She was stooped beside a small child in pigtails, blue overalls with no shirt and a baseball cap.

"Why not? It's true."

"Yes, I know. But you still shouldn't. Not just now anyway." She glanced in my direction.

I tried to smile, but my lips felt like slabs of concrete; they barely moved.

"Hi." She grinned with instant cheerfulness.

I attempted a return greeting, but only air came out.

She leaned toward the little girl, her smile frozen suspiciously in place, and whispered, "Quick! Go tell Dad he's awake!"

I tried to sit up, but a thousand shooting pains beginning at my toes and ending at my teeth stopped me cold. I forced my mouth to make a word.

"Mmph."

"Excuse me?"

"Mmmph, mmph, mpmph." One sentence, and my lips felt as though I'd just played the clarinet for three hours.

"I'm sorry. I can't get what you're saying."

"Mm-ph, mm-ph, mph-mph." A dog could speak clearer.

"Listen, if you could just wait a second, my dad will be here. He can understand."

Oh, yeah? Could he read concrete?

"Are you feeling better?"

"Phm, phm."

"How's your head?"

"Phmmuphmphmm."

"Are you hungry?"

I nodded at that important question.

"What sounds good to you?"

Fried chicken. "Mmph mphmph."

"Soup?"

I nodded again. It was better than nothing.

"Good morning." A man in a flannel shirt, jeans and heavy hiking boots walked into the room. His face, which was clean shaven, pale and rather drawn, did not match his mountaineering clothes. He had a short Hitler mustache, which I bet a million dollars his wife begged him regularly to cut off, and his eyebrows were thick enough to attract birds.

"Dad, he wants to eat!" the girl interrupted excitedly.

"That's good, Ed." Without taking his eyes off me, he waved her toward the door. "Why don't you open a can of broth? And, please, keep the others out for a while so the young man and I can get to know each other a little better."

She left obediently, and the man walked with exaggerated nonchalance to my bedside. "So how are we feeling today?"

"Mphhmph phom phomph."

"Your lips are too swollen to talk?"

How about that! He *could* read concrete.

He pulled a pad and pencil from a dresser drawer and handed it to me. "Write how you feel on this."

LIKE I DIDN'T JUMP OUT OF THE PLANE IN TIME.

He chuckled and nodded. "Do you have a headache?"

That was an understatement. My skull was throbbing hard enough to register on the Richter scale. The pain started at my nose and stretched all the way around my brain to the back of my neck.

YES.

"Would you like a painkiller?"

ARE YOU A DRUG DEALER?

He chuckled again. "No, son, a doctor."

WHAT HAPPENED TO ME?

His expression sobered, and his mustache shrank when his grin disappeared. "You fell from a tree."

Well, that explained why I wanted to scream every time I moved.

IT MUST HAVE BEEN ONE OF THE GIANT REDWOODS.

"My name is Dr. Eric Essig." The seconds ticked by. He studied me closely. "What's your name?"

My name? I thought about it for a moment. It was the craziest thing. Extremely weird, very confusing. *What was my name?*

Dr. Essig seemed to understand my frustration.

"Don't worry, son. It will undoubtedly come to you later. You see, you've suffered a minor concussion, and I'm afraid your nose has been dislocated. The jolt, and the following shock, has probably caused a temporary loss of memory."

AMNESIA?

"Perhaps. But it's nothing to be too concerned about. I'm sure it's just temporary. If I thought it was more serious, I would've had you flown to a hospital. However, your symptoms indicate that I can treat you just as effectively here."

As I stared at one of the huge yellow roses on my sheet, the strangest questions began seeping into my mind. Who was I? Why was I on top of a giant redwood? What time was it? Where was I supposed to be? What if my memory never came back? Did I have insurance to pay this guy? When would I be able to move my lips again?

What was my name?

"We took the liberty of checking your clothes in hopes of locating some sort of ID."

I glanced up curiously.

"We couldn't find any. Not even a wallet."

We studied each other in silence. A guy my age should've had some sort of identification. A library card, a parking ticket, a dry cleaning receipt, something.

"Do you usually carry your belongings in your pocket?"

PROBABLY.

"Do you recall owning a wallet?"

EVERYBODY HAS WALLETS.

"The reason I'm so concerned is that you probably have a family somewhere that's very worried about you. If we had an address or a phone number, we might be able to contact them."

I thought hard. It made my head pound.

SORRY.

"Okay, son. Don't worry about it now. We have a radio, and we've been listening to the news regularly. Someone is bound to report the balloon missing." He leaned closer to me, his eyes narrowing as if to scrutinize my innermost thoughts. "Do you remember your balloon?"

Somehow I knew he wasn't talking about the kind that you tie to a string. But other than that, I didn't know what he was getting at.

WHAT BALLOON?

"Soup's on!" The auburn-haired girl walked swiftly across the braided rug and stared at me with bright green eyes. "Do you remember me yet?"

Dr. Essig gave her a hard, scolding look.

"Oh. Sorry." She set a tray containing a bowl of broth, crackers and a cloth napkin on my lap.

"Fmph, fuumph, mumph." I handed her my pad. WHAT'S YOUR NAME?

"Edon. Ed for short. What's yours?" She cringed and peeked over her shoulder at her father. He frowned.

I attempted another smile, but I think it looked more like a sneer.

"Here. I'll feed you." She sat on the bed, making the soup slosh a little, and picked up a spoon.

I felt ultimately stupid, but it appeared to be the only way I was going to get anything into my stomach. My lips parted, and she poured the broth in.

"Does that taste good?"

I nodded. A starving man has no pride.

She scooped up another spoonful. "So tell me, where are you from?"

"Ed!"

"I mean, is it somewhere in the state?"

Dr. Essig motioned her from the room. Firmly.

If amnesia wasn't anything to be concerned about, why was he acting so self-consciously?

Edon waved to me before she closed the door, and I lifted a finger back at her. Suddenly I was very tired. Without intending to, I drifted away again.

Chapter Two

There were several interesting knickknacks to focus on in the rustically decorated den: an antique saddle, a Navaho blanket, a moose head, an enlarged photograph of the Grand Canyon. But I chose the tiny sailboat in the gooseneck bottle. It was like me in a way. Sailboats are often without destinies and have a useless sort of detachment from the world. They're different from boats that sport motors for direction. Even worse, they can only progress as fast as the wind allows them.

The midmorning sun streaming through the small open window was a merciless lure. I'd been bedridden in my makeshift bedroom for days, and I was sure the wind behind my sail had all but stopped. I was able to remain alert for longer periods of time now. Still, Dr. Essig, who'd become somewhat annoying with a collection of "rules for recovery" that seemed as thick as a dictionary, said I wasn't strong enough to walk yet. Especially outside. To pass the time, I found myself plotting all sorts of imaginary escapes.

Dr. Essig would come to chat and offer me an aspirin. While he was changing the dressing on my head, I would slip two or three of the pills into his coffee. He'd fall over, and I'd be gone like a whiff of air....

The only problems were that I didn't have enough pills, Dr. Essig didn't drink coffee, and he'd probably drop right on top of me. I'd yell, because I'm not very good with intense pain, and be caught by Edon, who'd become Dr. Essig's equally tough assistant.

Plan number two was a midnight breakout. I'd wait until the cabin was soundless and then simply take a stroll, maybe check out the balloon I'd supposedly landed in, and listen to the owls and the frogs while...

Unfortunately I couldn't stay conscious for more than an hour or two at a time. It would be difficult outlasting everyone in falling asleep. And even if I succeeded that far, I'd probably only make it halfway down the hall before my eyeballs turned in. If I landed on my nose again, Dr. Essig would probably have to remove it completely.

"Hi. Sorry it took so long. I wanted to make sure I got everything you asked for," Edon said, carrying the crowded tray carefully to the bed.

I'd met the entire Essig family now, except for Cristy, who everyone explained had trouble facing wounded people. I liked them all, but especially Edon. Even though she wouldn't give in to my objections any easier than her father, she was always around when I needed something. The faithful nurse.

"Are you sure you want this?" she asked, making a face. "Scrambled eggs with onions and catsup, toast with peanut butter, last night's hot German potato salad, and a bowl of Raisin Bran?"

"Milk?" I was more articulate with my speech now. I spoke slowly, concentrating on one syllable at a time. Melissa said I sounded like Frankenstein.

"Oh, yeah, and milk." She moved the glass to the front of the tray where I could see it.

"Looks deli-cious."

"To you maybe. Everyone else got sick when I showed them."

It didn't take long to consume most of what I'd asked for. My stomach was recovering better than any other part of my body.

Edon started to take the tray away. "Can I bring you something else?"

"A mirror. I want-to see-what I-look like."

She paused.

"Okay, but I have to check with Dad first. I'll be right back."

I made grumbling noises. Dr. Essig had to approve everything: what I could eat, how I should sleep, when I could move and even if I could look at myself. When I'd asked for a mirror once before, he'd replied that it "wasn't a good idea yet." He said the appearance of my face at this stage of recovery might discourage me. He thought my attitude was exemplary, considering all that had happened, and he wanted my spirits to remain high.

"Dad must be fishing," Ed reported. She closed the door behind her. "So I took it upon myself to permit this." She held up a hand mirror for my inspection.

"Thanks E-don." I positioned myself so I could see better and glanced at my reflection. It was awful! I yelped.

"Oh, come on. It's not that bad. You've improved a lot."

Not that bad? Was she serious? My face was puffy and purple and covered with iodine. My eyes were black, my hair was greasy enough to slide off my head, and I didn't have a nose.

"Creature-from the-lost bal-loon," I moaned. No wonder her sister never came in to talk to me.

I felt terrible.

"Now don't get upset." Edon tucked the mirror away. "This is all temporary."

"Yes, I know. Like-my memor-y."

"Oh, boy." She looked mildly panicked. "If you get depressed, Dad's going to hold me responsible. He's warned me a hundred times not to be so abrupt with you."

"Is there-a nose under-the band-age?"

"Yes, I'm sure there is . . . at least Dad never indicated otherwise. And, like I said, everything will get back to normal again." She hesitated. "You know, you were pretty cute before you fell on your face."

I moaned again.

"Blond, blue eyes, nice tan. Cristy said, 'Look at the fox in that balloon!' when she saw you coming. And Cristy is an expert on the appearance of the opposite sex. She doesn't call anyone cute unless they're Bruce Springsteen's level or above." She shrugged. "We both think you're cute."

"Have they-said any-thing on-the ra-dio?"

"No. Not yet."

I glanced at the sailboat.

"Hey!" Edon was trying her best to sound cheerful. "Did you know that only two or three guys have ever flown over the Grand Canyon in a balloon?"

I shook my head.

"One man got permission to do it as a business. He thought taking tourists back and forth across the Canyon in a balloon would be a great way to get rich. On the first ride, he couldn't find an air current to get him across. On the second ride, the wind kept slamming him into the canyon wall. He broke a couple of bones, and it scared him so bad that he sold his balloon and hasn't gone up since."

I squinted my eyes skeptically.

"It's true," she insisted. She leaned forward, her green eyes wide with curiosity. "Did you fly across the Canyon before you came here?"

"I don't think-so. It would-be sui-cide."

She looked disappointed. "Dad says you had to be a pretty good pilot to land in such high winds."

"Oh, yeah. Look at-me."

"No, no. You don't understand. Your landing was good. The tree limbs weren't strong enough to hold you up. That's all." She watched me quietly for a while. It was long enough to make me wonder what she was thinking.

"You're going to have to give us a name one of these days."

"You want-me to-make one-up?"

"Sure. We'll never know what to call you otherwise."

It was so weird. My life was upside down and backwards. How many guys choose their own names? How many guys *have* to choose their own names? "Rick Spring-steen."

She smiled. "That's pretty conceited."

"You said-I was-cute."

"How about Frankie?"

"Am I Ita-lian?"

"No."

"Ro-bert Red-ford."

"Too old. How about Hans?"

Feeling tired, I sighed and closed my eyes. Why was it I could remember everyone else's name but my own?

"We could call him Wayne!" The door opened, and a guilty eavesdropper stuck her rosy-cheeked face in.

"Melissa!" Edon scolded, pulling her the rest of the way into the room. "You shouldn't spy on people!"

"Mommy said I could stand by the door. Besides, I want to help name him."

"He's not your pet, Melissa."

"I vote Wayne. Let's call him Wayne!"

"I told you," Edon said, her voice growing soft but tense. "We can't name him Wayne, so stop saying it."

Melissa pouted, her eyes darkened with disappointment.

I wanted to tell them that I didn't care what they called me, but I couldn't find the energy. Three seconds later, I was out.

It was like a scene from a family photo album. Dr. Essig had his arm draped over Mrs. Essig's shoulder. Cristy, who I'd discovered was an undeniable babe, stood in front of her mother. Edon fidgeted restlessly in front of Dr. Essig, and Melissa was squeezed between her two sisters.

They applauded enthusiastically when I stepped onto the wooden porch. I covered my eyes with one arm and waved the other wildly in front of me, imitating how Frankenstein might act if he'd just been released from his dungeon. They loved it. I clomped my feet on the steps, and Mrs. Essig started jumping up and down, shouting for me to hold still while she took a picture.

I put two fists in the air and began doo-doo-dooing to the theme song of *Rocky*. Melissa started giggling and acting so silly that Dr. Essig told her to quiet down or return to the cabin.

"How does it feel to be outside?" Edon asked from their small congregation in the clearing.

"Great! Doo-doo-dooo, do-do-dooo…"

"Now take those steps carefully," Dr. Essig warned.

"Stop on the bottom for another picture," Mrs. Essig said, keeping her camera aimed.

"The point of this Martha, is to help him get exercise, not his portrait."

"Pictures are important, Eric."

"Hey, Mr. Jock, wanna race?"

"Ed!"

"It's not a bad word, Mom."

"Yeah, I'll race. Tie your big toes together and we'll start from here."

"She should tie her big lips together," Cristy snapped.

"Not too fast young man!"

"Hold it right there!" Mrs. Essig moved in clicking.

"Doo-doo-dooo…"

"All right, that's enough Melissa. Now go inside!"

"Ahhh, Dad, she's just excited," Cristy said.

"How's the right leg feel son?"

"About the same as the left. Two wet sponges."

"Sure you don't want to race?" Edon asked, laughing.

"Go get the string."

"Now give us a big smile. Just one more. Say fleas!"

"Good grief, Martha! Would you put that thing down!"

And so it went. My first walk over twenty feet, and you would've thought I was skydiving from the edge of the earth. Although the Essig family could be trying at times like this, I couldn't help but appreciate their genuine concern. I doubted that many other families would've shown such kindness to a stranger. They were united, too. Husband, wife, kids.

"Okay! Everyone back into the house for kitchen detail. On the double!" Dr. Essig ordered. It was funny. I knew he'd never been in the service, but he was always acting like a drill sergeant. I guess raising three girls is what did it to him.

"Eric! You're not intending to leave him alone out here, are you?" Mrs. Essig exclaimed, finally dropping the camera from her face.

"Of course not, dear. Ed will stay with him. She's become a trustworthy nurse, wouldn't you say, son?"

"Absolutely." I grinned, crossing my fingers for only Edon to see.

"Can I watch him, too?" Melissa's brown eyes became round and pleading.

"No." Cristy looked at Edon. "One person slithering out of dishes is enough."

"I'd hardly call caring for an injured man slithering out of anything," Edon observed defensively. "He doesn't exactly eat like a mouse you know." I felt my ears growing hot. She squared her shoulders proudly. "There's a lot more to nursing than fluffing pillows."

"Yeah. Like wooing and gooing over the patient."

"Cristy!"

"Well, at least I care," Edon snapped.

"Yes, Little Miss Cinderella Nightingale. And is it my fault I can't take the sight of someone so...so..." Cristy stopped herself and glanced at me. "I'm sorry. Cuts and things, well, they just make me feel sick."

I nodded, releasing her from her bondage of guilt. It would've been great if they had just dropped the subject.

"What Cristy says is true," Mrs. Essig testified. "She'd make a great model, or fashion designer, but we've given up all hopes of her ever becoming a surgeon."

I'd say so. But Cristy's beauty made up for any minor shortcomings as far as I was concerned. I really couldn't blame her either. It took courage for me to look at my face, too, and I belonged to it. Although the scratches were smaller, the bandage on my nose was shrinking, and my eyes were now pastel plum instead of black, it was still the leftovers of a bloody accident.

"I'm sorry," Edon apologized when we were alone. "Cristy and I sometimes get into it."

"That's normal."

"She's been especially grouchy since we arrived at the cabin."

"Where do you live when you're not here?"

"Phoenix."

"Do you stay at the Grand Canyon every summer?"

"This is the first time. Dad thought it would be a good idea for all of us to get away together. He picked the perfect spot, too. No telephone, no TV. The only ways to get in and out of here are by a miracle, your feet or a Jeep."

"What happens in case of an emergency?"

"You've been our only emergency. But with Dad being a doctor and all we didn't have to radio for a helicopter."

"A helicopter!" I exclaimed in surprise. "Is that the only way to get out?"

"Until August 31 it is. That's when Dad arranged for the guide to come back. In the meantime, if anything happens, we have to radio the Coronado National Forest Service."

"But what about food?"

"That *would* be your first concern." Edon laughed teasingly. "But not to worry. We've got tons of it. As long as you don't mind powdered eggs and powdered milk."

"Is that what I've been eating?"

"You couldn't taste the difference?"

"Only when you forgot to add the water."

Edon shaded her eyes to see me. "You think it's crazy living all the way out here, don't you?"

"Kind of. Men like your father aren't usually away from their practices so long. I'm sure he has a good reason for it, though."

She kicked a pebble with her toe. "He does."

We listened to the chatter of an angry squirrel for a few seconds, neither of us speaking. Edon swung around suddenly. "Hey! Would you like to see the basket that dumped you on your face?"

Sweet, delicate Edon. "Do you always describe things so graphically?"

"Sure. Except for your—you know—your problem."

Amnesia. Yes, even Edon avoided the subject. The Essigs brought no more attention to it than they would someone's missing hand or foot. I'll admit that it wasn't comfortable to live with. The confusing disorientation I would sometimes suffer was as frustrating as trying to jog in a dark closet.

"It's over here." She led me around the south side of the cabin where tufts of seeding grasses and patches of buttercups were thick under the sun. The smell of pine freshened my senses. A blue jay sounded a shrill alert at our sudden presence, and two chipmunks scurried out of sight.

It felt great to be outside. It was even more exciting to finally see something that was mine. The big suede-rimmed gondola was a link to my identity, and a clue to my past. It was the one item, my only possession to even recognize. Dr. Essig said one recollection might lead to another. It could even jolt my memory into functioning again.

I studied it carefully, letting my fingers trail along the wicker sides. I grabbed a bar and started to swing my leg over the top.

"You're not going to try to get in there!" Edon spouted with alarm.

"And why not?"

"You're just now walking. Risking a broken neck comes next week."

"I'm fine," I assured her, hopping inside before she could object further.

"Now look what you've done!" she scolded. "You're in it!"

"That's right. And still alive. Care to join me?" I stretched my hand to her.

"Could I?" The twinkle in her eyes denied her responsible position as nurse and gave way to the adventurer. She started to take my hand but stopped and grabbed a bar instead. "I'm not going to risk pulling you over and giving you another broken nose," she explained.

"Don't flatter yourself. My leg alone makes two of you."

"Yeah, but it's made of sponge. You admitted it yourself."

"Steel-like sponge. Did I neglect to say steel-like?" She laughed.

"Do you like to fly?" I asked.

"I think I'd love it." She peered at the ground, probably wondering what it would be like to look down from the heavens. "I've read about ballooning, and they had a balloon festival in Phoenix last year. They're so-o-o huge and grand looking!"

"So you've never been up?"

"Excuse me, Mr. Airmale, but it's too embarrassing to beg a ride. And I don't know anyone who owns one."

"You do now. By the way, where's the envelope?"

"It's in the cellar. We packed it as carefully as we could. We did the opposite of the people at the festival when they unpacked theirs. Pulled it out, then rolled it up. We didn't see any damage, but, then, we didn't know what we were looking for."

"I really appreciate the way your family has taken care of everything. You're nice people."

"It's no big deal. What's that?" She pointed to the instrument panel.

"The variometer. It tells you whether you're going up or down, and how fast. This is the altimeter. It tells you how high you are above the ground."

"And what's this supposed to be?"

"That's the owner's plaque."

I paused, blinking at it dumbly.

"The owner's plaque!" Bending so that my broken nose was only a few inches away, I stared at the indented square.

"What's it say? Can you see it? What's it say?" Edon chattered above me.

I straightened, feeling even more confused and puzzled then usual. "Someone has removed it."

"Maybe it fell off when you crashed."

"No. Something like this doesn't just drop off."

"Maybe it was never there in the first place. Do you remember if it was ever on?"

I sighed. "No. Like the rest, it's a blank." Nothing was ever in focus. I could depend on my mind the way a fish could swim across the desert.

"Well, don't get depressed about it." She made her voice high and perky like a Disneyland tour guide. "Dad says you'll be getting your memory back pretty soon. Hey! I have a great idea! You want to have lunch in the balloon?"

Good ol' Edon. She never let me think about the heavy stuff too long. "Sure. But it's only been a couple of hours since breakfast."

"That's right. Your normal pattern of dining."

"Funny." I tweaked her cheek. "How old are you anyway? If you're under thirty-nine, I'm going to throw you out."

"I'm nearly fifteen. How old are—" She stopped herself. "Sorry."

"Don't worry about it. How old do you think I am?" I flexed my arms and collected myself into a muscle man stance. "Twenty-two or twenty-three?"

She looked skeptical. "I think twenty would be pushing it. Does nineteen sound more familiar?"

"Twenty-one."

"You're not twenty-one! You don't even shave yet."

"Yeah, but I drink. Where's my whiskey anyway?" I pounded the rim with my fist.

"Don't be a simpleton."

"I've thought of a name for myself, too, so you guys won't be calling me Hey, He and Him all the time."

"Good. What is it?"

"Columbus."

"Columbus?"

"You may refer to me as Column for short."

She made a face. "That's terrible!"

"All right. How about Mason?"

"As in Perry?"

"Well, since I'm trying to dig up facts all the time, it seems fitting."

"Perry?"

"No. Mason. I don't like Perry."

"I think it suits you."

"Wonderful. I'm twenty-one years old. Mason Redford from Moscow."

"Do you speak Russian?"

"I doubt it."

She started to climb out of the basket. "I don't know, Mason, people might get suspicious if you say you're from the Soviet Union and you can't speak Russian. Will you be okay in here while I get our lunch?"

"Sure. I feel fine."

"Do you promise not to climb out, or faint, while I'm gone, in case you might smash up your face again?"

"Promise. Give my word. Sign in blood."

She threw me an "all right I'm trusting you on your life so you better do or die" kind of look before she jogged around the corner of the cabin. Restrictions were becoming fairly common to me. I was restricted from strolling too fast, restricted from staying awake too long, restricted from breathing through my nose and restricted from knowing more than this small acre of trees. I could certainly handle being confined in my basket for a few minutes. I decided to concentrate on the gondola again. I messed with the trigger on the blast valve for a while and then checked over the tanks.

No sudden memory return.

I studied the empty square where the owner's plaque was supposed to be, trying to figure out what could've happened to it. The plaque had been there once; there were enough marks to make it obvious. Deciding I should look for it, just in case Edon was right about it being knocked loose, I began feeling every possible pocket and hidden corner where it might've fallen. Instead, I discovered an empty champagne bottle that had its cork replaced. It was tucked inconspicuously in the console, and it was the only loose object in the gondola.

Maybe I really did drink.

I pulled the cork and, to my surprise, I found a string attached. It had been needled through and knotted at the top, so that whatever was hooked on below would come out when the cork was lifted.

Carefully I pulled it up. A money roll dangled before my eyes. It was bound so tightly that it was bullet hard.

So Mason Redford from Moscow had some cold cash. That was encouraging! I took off the outer bands and was forced to stop breathing as the first bill uncurled from the roll. It was a five-thousand-dollar number! It was so amazing that I had to count the zeros twice to be sure. Instantly sensitive to the wind, I tucked it quickly into my jeans and unwrapped another. Five thousand again! I clutched my heart.

Two more.

Three. All of them five-thousand-dollar bills! When I was finished, I had to sit down from the shock of my sudden wealth. One hundred thousand dollars. A note was tucked in the center of it.

THE FINDER OF THIS SHOULD NEVER FORGET THAT MONEY IS A POOR SUB-STITUTE FOR LOVE. WEALTH WAS MEANT TO BE SHARED. IF NOT, YOU

HAVE NOTHING, AND YOU ARE INDEED A
POOR MAN.

What kind of friends did I have? Did I even know
the person who'd written it?

Who was I?

The morning was whispering a promise of a wonderful day. If the sky was wet, it could've passed for
the Mediterranean Sea. It was the deepest blue of any
I'd ever seen. And the forest was loud with life. There
must've been a thousand varieties of birds, judging by
the different songs clashing from the treetops. The
underlying breeze seemed to be carrying the same
message to all of us. It was great to be alive!

And why not? I was a hundred thousand dollars
richer. I respected the philosophy of the person who'd
written the note, but it was hard to deny its usefulness
to a homeless guy like myself.

A gift that substantial doesn't just drop into someone's life like a pair of cuff links either. A person needs
to appreciate the little favors he runs into.

I glanced at my cheap digital watch and faded jeans.
Obviously I was the sort of boy who had lots of room
for appreciation.

Swinging rhythmically back and forth on the
wooden porch swing, listening to the sounds of the
canyon, I found it easy to continue counting my
blessings. I could've crashed in the city. Having amnesia was disorienting enough when things around me
were simple. To suffer through it in the whirl of a
bustling city, where a person can get lost even with all
his brain parts intact, would've been *high anxiety.*

And then there were the Essigs. What a great family! They functioned like clockwork. They tried so hard to keep things light and happy. A Swiss Family Robinson with a sense of earnestness to match the Waltons, and here I was, fortunate enough to land in their midst.

I could've crashed on the lawn of a guy who wasn't so friendly. I might've gone to jail for crushing someone's gardenias, smashing someone's fence, or double-parking on someone's fireplace. I'm sure the actual number of people who would've taken me into their home was almost nonexistent. And to end up with a doctor besides! Who could've asked for anything more?

I turned the bottled sailboat slowly between my fingers. Like everything else, the Essigs didn't mind that I was treating the craft as my own. It made me feel guilty about hiding my new wealth from them, as if I were being ungratefully deceptive about it.

But a hundred thousand dollars! How do you explain that much cash? Especially with amnesia?

Then there was the matter of the missing plaque. The more I thought about it, the more certain I was that someone had removed it. Of course, it was just a feeling I had, but when a person doesn't possess a memory, that's all he can go on.

"Good morning, Mason." Cristy gave me a straight, white smile and walked to the swing, brushing her long shiny hair. Her attractiveness was a recurring phenomenon to me, as it probably was to every other male under twenty in the universe. She'd become increasingly friendly toward me as my recovery progressed, making rich Mason Redford a happy, healing boy.

"Are you heading out this morning?" I asked.

"In a few minutes. Dad's packing some things, and Mom's trying to find more film. She wants to get a picture of your first hike."

I laughed. "Your mom and dad are really something. You're fortunate to have them."

She flipped her hair behind her shoulders. "I'm not so sure."

"Hey, come on! They're like the foster parents from an orphan movie."

"Oh, right. And I'm supposed to be the happy heiress."

"Correct. Look at all the great things around you." I waved my hands in every general direction.

"What? You mean this prison?"

"Be real, Cristy. A lot of kids would like to spend a summer here."

"You don't know." Her pretty face clouded over. "Our family isn't as perfect as you think. Dad wanted us to show our 'good sides to you' to keep from upsetting you until you were more stable."

"Well, I'm more stable now, and everyone's the same."

"It's only a matter of time."

I pursed my lips contemplatively, then shook my head. "No, you guys have real kinship. You're different. You just haven't looked around at other people."

"Pulleeese, Mason. You have us sounding like the model home. Mr. and Mrs. Harmony and family."

"That's how I see it."

"What about Ed and me? We seem to argue all the time these days."

"Sibling rivalry. Perfectly normal. Another thing I've noticed is how generous your parents are. They're very nice. Your dad is not even going to bill me for his care."

"I should hope not. That would be uncivil." She lifted her perfectly formed chin proudly.

"Your mom treats me like one of the family."

"That's only proper etiquette."

"Exactly what I mean, Cristy. You aren't aware of how concerned they are about others."

"Oh, now *that* I do know." She began to brush her hair harder. "And it may be an endearing quality for a while, but try living with it for a year. You might not be so impressed or understanding."

"Mason! Oooooh, Maaaason..." Edon burst through the door and started to sail off the porch until she caught sight of me out of the corner of her eye. She froze, pivoted on her heel and opened her mouth to speak. She noticed Cristy was with me and clamped her mouth shut again.

"Are we ready?" I asked.

"Almost. Melissa can't find her other tennis shoe." She strolled to the railing that bordered the porch and leaned against it, her manner switching from frantic to casual.

Cristy clunked her brush down on the swing. "Well, why don't you help her?"

"Why don't you?" Ed shot back.

"I'm busy brushing my hair."

"And do you think you'll be done sometime this year?"

Cristy shrugged. "I don't want to fight with you."

That sounded good to me. I considered sibling rivalry to be pretty normal stuff, but it bothered me when Cristy and Edon went at it. "So this great trout stream Doc keeps talking about, where is it?" I asked.

"If you don't want to fight, then why do you always take shots at everyone?" Edon inquired, determined to prove a point.

"Me!" Cristy blinked her eyes in exaggerated wonderment. "You're the one who's always choosing sides with Mom and Dad."

"Did it ever occur to you that you're not always right?" Ed folded her arms authoritatively.

"Oh. So you think smothering us to death is all right?"

"No, but I don't see how arguing constantly helps anything."

"You're too immature to know."

"Is someone getting the fishing poles?" I glanced back and forth between them.

"And at the age of seventeen, you're the fountain of knowledge!"

"I comprehend more than you."

"At least you think you do."

"How about worms? Do we have worms?"

Cristy jumped up glaring. "Wayne used to stick by me in everything. And I stuck by him!"

"He wouldn't have battled with Mom and Dad the way you do! He never did!"

"He'd stand up for what he thought was right."

"But you aren't right! All you think about is yourself. It doesn't help Mom and Dad when they have to worry about you all the time, too."

"At least I'm trying to get things back to normal. You tiptoe around as though we're living in a box of eggs. Wayne is gone!"

"Who's Wayne?"

They both stopped and turned to stare at me. "What?"

"Who's this guy Wayne?"

"I found it! I found it!" Melissa burst through the door, waving a red sneaker triumphantly in the air. "It's time to go. Smile, Mason. Mommy's taking your picture!"

Mrs. Essig trotted out the door and lifted her camera in front of my face. She clicked, a bulb flashed and I was blinded.

"It's daylight, Mrs. Essig," I complained, blinking as two white polka dots formed in my center vision.

"I know, Mason, but I want to make sure some of these pictures come out. I didn't mean to startle you."

"It's okay."

"Do you mind if I take another?"

"Who? Me?"

She aimed, clicked and the white polka dots shot into a white wall. "Please, Mason, I've asked you before to call me Martha. You're too much a part of the family for Mrs. Essig!"

"Okay. If I ever see again, I'll call you Martha."

Laughing, she reached down and hugged me. At least I thought she was the one who was hugging me.

"Man the boats and warn the fish! Eric Essig is hungry for trout!" Dr. Essig bellowed from the front door.

"Daddy!" Melissa scolded. "You aren't really going to eat our friends the fish, are you?"

He laughed uneasily. "Perhaps we should discuss that matter more in-depth as we hike to the stream. Maybe Mommy would be willing to explain a few facts on the practicality of finned creatures."

"No, no, dear. Since you're the one who's so fond of the sport, it would be more appropriate for you to discuss the subject with your youngest child who, I would like to remind you, has three very close you-know-what friends swimming happily around in her you-know-what bowl at home."

"Point well-taken, Martha." He patted Melissa on the head, more or less chickening out for the moment, and stepped over to me. "Well, Mason, do you feel up to carrying the tackle box?"

"Sure, Doc." I adjusted the bandage on my nose. "I'm as tough as the next guy."

"Don't worry. I'll help him," Ed assured everyone.

We started for the stream. Mrs. Essig began pointing out different types of butterflies and the many varieties of birds. Dr. Essig teased that she'd been watching too many wildlife documentaries, and Mrs. Essig replied that he was just jealous because he'd once tried to feed acorns to a brown skunk that he'd mistaken for an "odd-looking squirrel."

Edon and Cristy remained abnormally quiet. Dr. Essig soon noticed and began to focus his attention on them, determined to get his two reluctant daughters to adopt a better attitude for the family outing. Nothing he tried worked. Evidently the argument they had had on the porch was more serious than it had sounded. Neither one seemed able to break out of her smoldering mood.

When we reached the stream, things were near an erupting point. I could tell for several reasons. Edon was kicking every stone near her, Cristy's chin was rising higher than her nose, and Dr. Essig had suddenly stopped speaking, and yet his mustache continued to move.

He handed each of us a bag of salmon eggs for bait. Cristy refused hers.

"I don't feel like fishing, Dad," she said.

"Of course you do," he replied.

"No, Dad, I really don't."

"He's been fixing the poles for us since dawn," Edon cut in, glaring at her sister.

"That's really nice, E-don. Why don't you take mine, and then you'll have two?" Cristy's pretty face was becoming hard with tension. "I told Dad last night I'd rather stay at the cabin and read a book, but he wouldn't listen."

"Honey, do you really think Cristy has to fish if she doesn't want to?" Mrs. Essig looked worried.

"Yes, Martha. I want her to enjoy herself."

"Then let me read a book and skip the hooks and eggs and smelly fish."

Dr. Essig sighed. "Okay. If you insist on missing out on all the fun we've planned for today, then you're excused. But just this once."

"May I go back to the cabin?"

"Absolutely not. Not by yourself."

"But, Dad," she whined. "I don't want to sit out here swatting at gnats."

"Sorry, Cristy. Going back alone is too dangerous."

"Like how? I might get gored by a buffalo? Or maybe knocked around by a lost mugger?"

"Don't get smart with your father," Mrs. Essig warned.

"Well there's nothing that can happen out here in the middle of nowhere!"

What was happening to the Swiss Family Robinson with the qualities of the Waltons to match? I could scarcely believe my eyes.

"You heard what your father said."

"Paranoid. You guys are paranoid."

"Cristy, shut up!" Edon interrupted.

"But they are!"

"Don't talk to us that way young lady! You lower your voice."

"I can't breathe around you."

"We're only looking out for your own good."

"Are you? Or are you just trying to keep yourselves from getting hurt again?"

"Shut up, Cristy!" Edon repeated.

"We're your parents. What do you expect from us?"

"To breathe." Her eyes grew watery. "That's all. Just to get some air."

Mrs. Essig became tearful, too, followed by Edon, and then Melissa, who was too scared to know what else to do. Dr. Essig's expression turned grimmer than an executioner's.

The perfect home had just cracked before my eyes.

Stupid Mason Redford from Moscow. Why hadn't I noticed before that the Essigs had a problem. One that went all the way to the heart. As we walked in single file down the grass-trodden path to the cabin, absolutely silent, I had plenty of time to think that question over. Maybe, as Cristy had indicated, they had been hiding it from me. Maybe I'd been so absorbed by my own problems that I couldn't see anyone else's. Or maybe I just didn't want to face it. Running around without any connection to the past, not knowing who you are or where you belong, can be unnerving. It was comforting thinking of the Essigs as a solid family unit I could depend on.

Naturally I quickly became the outsider. When a family is doing well, it's easy to include others in their lives. But look out when the hard times hit! They ball up like armadillos. I wanted to help, which was more upsetting than anything else because I couldn't. Something was going on that I didn't know about, and since no one was jumping at the gate to tell me what it was, I was as lost as they were.

I knew this guy Wayne could help me with a few facts. I'd heard enough about him to guess that he was pretty close to the Essigs.

And, also, that he was no longer around to talk to.

That left Edon as the best source for getting to the bottom of things. She was smart for her age, more together in some ways than Cristy, who was three years older. I knew she wouldn't mind answering some questions, even if they were personal. She didn't feel inhibited about quizzing me on anything. That was for sure.

When we reached the cabin, we all went to our separate rooms. Things stayed quiet the rest of the day, through dinner and into the night. Dr. Essig talked to Cristy in her room and then moved on to Edon's.

There was no more shouting or arguing. It had become very still.

And somehow sad.

It was well into the next week before I got a chance to talk to Edon alone. She was trying to console me on not hearing anything about a runaway balloon on the radio. Dr. Essig had made contact with the Flagstaff Police Station, asking about any missing person reports that might fit my description and, like every other lead we'd thought of, it led to a dead end. No one seemed to be making any efforts to find me. Edon was still trying to convince me that it was just a matter of time. She was using her usual tact, and it might've depressed me if I hadn't been more concerned with her family's problem than my own situation.

"I'm sure there's someone out there who's missing you. Only bums and winos don't have people looking for them," Edon pointed out, pushing the porch swing to a higher speed with the tips of her toes.

"Thanks, Edon."

"I know you're not a bum. Your hair's too short."

"What about a wino?"

"Naw. You would've experienced withdrawal symptoms. Besides, winos live in gutters, not balloons."

"Can I ask you a question?" We'd finished dinner a few minutes ago, and I knew Melissa would be hunting me out for a piggyback ride any second.

Realizing my tone was serious, she slowed the porch swing and looked at me. "Sure. Except if it's about Cristy. I don't like to answer your questions about Cristy."

"It's about all of you. Let me see, maybe I can put this delicately. There's something that's been bothering me." I paused. "I'm not sure how to say it. It's a subject that's very hard to put into words—"

"You want to know why we all blew up at the creek the other day."

I shook my head. "You're really something."

"Oh, yeah? If you truly believed that, then why are you always looking at Cristy?"

"Who's always looking at Cristy?"

"You. Like your eyeballs don't have lids."

"Oh, come on. I don't look at her that much. And, besides, it's normal for guys to notice girls."

"Then why don't you notice me the same way you notice her? I'm a girl. You can ask my mom."

"I don't know, Ed." I was growing uncomfortable with the direction of our conversation. "Because you dress differently, I guess. She wears pink blouses, and you wear army-olive T-shirts."

"But I don't like frilly things."

"Then don't buy them. All I know is some clothes are hard to ignore."

"I'm comfortable in overalls."

"Good. Look, Edon, you said you didn't mind if I asked a personal question. I asked it. Now you're supposed to answer it."

"You didn't ask it. I did. You couldn't think of a delicate way—"

"All right," I interrupted, frustrated. "Just tell me, will you? What, exactly, happened at the creek?"

The swing creaked rhythmically in the sudden silence. She lifted her toes from the floor planks, and we slowly rocked to a stop. Her eyes, which usually sparkled like marble-sized emeralds, clouded to a melancholy dullness. "It's not that easy to talk about," she said quietly.

It was unlike Edon to sound so sad. My chest swelled in responsive concern. "Come on. You can talk about anything," I said, attempting to lighten it up.

"Yeah. Usually." She gave a feeble sort of laugh and then swallowed. "Okay. Here goes. Do you remember when you asked Cristy and me who Wayne was?"

"Sure. That was the day you had the fight."

She nodded. "Well, you see, the guy we were talking about was my brother."

My heart tightened. "You don't have to say anything else if you don't want to," I whispered.

"No, that's okay." She took a deep breath. "Wayne was killed in a dirt bike accident a year ago. He was a really nice guy." She gazed at me solemnly. "Really. He was between Cristy and me and very funny and real bright and happy, and I don't know, we all miss him so much, well, it's just too awful." She started to cry very softly. We sat quietly for a while until she'd finished wiping the tears from her cheeks.

"You see, none of us are adjusting very well," she began again. "We've flunked every consciousness-encounter course Dad's enrolled us in. Especially he and Mom. Maybe it was because Wayne was their only son. I'm not sure. But they're having an awful time of it. Mom still cries at a word, and Dad, well, I've walked into his den more than a few times and seen tears in his eyes, too."

"It's not easy when someone you love dies." At that moment I felt pretty sad, too.

She sighed. "Yeah. Mom and Dad are trying. I mean, we just can't give up."

I didn't say anything.

"And poor Cristy and I. We never got along very well to begin with. Wayne was always our mediator. The peacemaker. Without him, we don't know how to be friends." She leaned over the arm of the swing to gaze through the screen door in fear that someone might overhear us. "I know Cristy misses Wayne as much as I do. She's lost without someone to back her up in her issues with Mom and Dad. Plus, she could talk to Wayne about personal things. She doesn't do that with me."

"Maybe it just takes a while."

"I get so mad at her, though. Now is no time to be forcing her independence. Mom and Dad are still so upset. She doesn't seem to care about anyone but herself. Like, who really cares if she walks back to the cabin by herself? Did she have to make such a big thing about it?"

I rubbed my chin thoughtfully, remembering that she'd called the cabin a prison. "Maybe she thinks your parents are too restrictive."

"Too restrictive?" Edon gave an incredulous laugh. "Are you kidding? They're like wardens. They treat us as though we have some terminal disease, and that if we bump ourselves too hard, we'll end up in the hospital."

"Or in a grave," I said quietly.

"That's what I mean. I know it's because of Wayne that they're acting so protective. They were never like this before. I think Cristy should be more patient with them. I hate it when she uses words like 'smothering' and 'ball and chain.' That's why I get so mad at her.''

Edon looked as if she expected me to express an opinion, but there was nothing to say. I could understand everyone's position. They each had good reasons for feeling the way they did, and no one person could be blamed for the trouble.

"It sort of all changed when you came along." She was smiling at me, her eyes clear again.

"Me?"

"You gave us something more to worry about."

"Yeah? I'm just that kind of guy."

"You helped us get our minds off Wayne. You looked in worse shape than anything we'd ever seen."

"Right. Creature from the Black Balloon."

"I don't think Dad's idea about us living at this lost cabin was working out until you dropped in." She poked me with her elbow. "Get it? *Dropped in?*"

"Yeah, yeah. Funny."

"I'm sure that's why Dad decided to keep you here instead of transferring you to a hospital. He could make a diagnosis from your symptoms, so why not?" She relaxed. "Anyway, I hate to say it, but your coming here was the best thing that's happened to us in a long, long time."

I nodded, beginning to see the irony of it all myself. "Yes, I suppose I couldn't have landed in a more opportune place for a lot of reasons. But what about your dad's practice? Isn't it kind of risky taking off for the entire summer?"

Edon began pushing the swing with her feet. "Dad's got a great reputation. He's a specialist in three related fields. I think he could be gone a whole year and his patients still wouldn't leave him.'' She turned to me, looking thoughtful. ''But even if it might hurt his practice, he still would've come. He knew things weren't right, and his family is more important to him. He would've forced us all here no matter what the obstacles.''

That fact was becoming as obvious to me as flowers are to bees. Now that I knew the past, I was assured even more that the Essigs were a special family.

Throughout the following month, I would spend more time getting to know them and less time staring at the sailboat, wondering who I was. I'd stay so busy, I'd forget that I even had amnesia.

Chapter Three

It's picture time, it's picture time!" Melissa sang out as she skipped in a circle around me.

Alert to sudden danger, I peered over my shoulders toward the kitchen and then to the hall. "What's up?" I whispered to my small, excited comrade.

She stretched to her tiptoes to reply conspiringly in my ear. "Daddy's going to take your nose off, and Mommy wants pictures of it."

"Pain City! Do you think I should try to escape?"

She giggled merrily. "Yes! If you can't be brave, then run! Run out the window, and I'll help you hide!"

I grabbed her small fingers, deciding that a plan of evacuation was indeed the wisest, and we scampered for the door.

"Coward!" Edon hooked her hands to her waist and shook her head disgustedly. "And teaching my baby sister to be chicken, too. Have you no sense of shame? Of valor?"

"Oh, yeah? You face your mom's mighty flashes sometime. I don't know what brand she uses, but my pupils scream whenever they see her camera." I picked Melissa up and carried her to the couch. "Anyhow, now that we're caught, we'll be brave. Right, Melissa?"

"Right, Mason. We won't cry when Daddy takes your nose off. Not even one tear."

"He's not going to take his nose off, Melissa, honey," Cristy explained, coming into the room with Mrs. Essig. "Daddy's just going to remove the bandage. You see, Mason's nose is all fixed now. There's no reason to wear it anymore."

Dr. Essig was soon to follow. He walked over, clicking some kind of surgical scissors in the air. "Want a local anesthetic first?"

Mrs. Essig ducked in front of me and flashed. "Pictures are much better when you catch your subject off guard. They're more natural."

"It's probably better if you don't see how Dad's artwork turned out anyway," Edon whispered close to my ear.

"That's right. Take advantage of a guy when he's down. Where's that anesthetic, Doc?" I heard Mrs. Essig positioning herself for an additional close-up. "Another picture, Mrs. Essig, and you guys will have to train a Seeing Eye wolf for me."

"Oh, all right, Mason," she conceded reluctantly. "I'll only take four or five more."

"A momentous compromise, Martha." Dr. Essig came closer and lifted my chin with his finger. "Okay, son, let's take a look at it. Let's see what kind of damage I've done to that handsome face of yours."

It sure was great the way everyone always joked about Dr. Essig's surgical abilities. They so amusingly saved it for times like these, too. Especially Dr. Essig himself. He'd drop his scissors very clumsily and say, "Whoops! I'll learn how to hold on to those things one of these days," or "I shouldn't have been messing around in that motor oil before I came in here. Hand me that rag and say, 'Ah.'"

What a comedian.

"Okay, son, show me where your nose is."

I played along, lifting my finger between my eyebrows, and Mrs. Essig flashed again.

Dr. Essig began his outpatient operation, and the room fell silent. I heard five different people breathing above me. As my vision returned, I saw five faces staring down like a circle of white balloons. Their eyes faded in first, followed quickly by their smiles.

"Mirror," Dr. Essig commanded with an upturned palm.

Edon slapped the tool in place, and he held it in front of me. "Okay, son, we're ready for inspection. Sorry I couldn't have situated things a little more in the center."

"His nose is still there!" Melissa shouted joyfully.

"Why, you look the same as when you first landed," Cristy observed, coming to sit on the couch beside me.

Mrs. Essig's camera flashed.

"What do you think?" Dr. Essig asked.

"From what I could see before Mrs. Essig blasted my eyeballs, it looked fine, Doc. You'll have to wait till my pupils float back up for details, though."

"Now don't get bitter, Mason, dear," Mrs. Essig said. "It isn't pretty, and frown lines don't look good on film."

"Is that the same nose he had before he fell out of his balloon?" Melissa asked.

"Of course, silly." Edon came to sit on the other side of me. "Now you're completely fixed, Mason. Your whole head is back to normal except for the brain part."

"And that will be coming soon enough," Dr. Essig said quickly.

"Sure. Anytime now," I replied, sounding as matter-of-fact about it as Edon, whose expression was now overloaded with guilt. I poked her with my elbow and whispered, "I got a reason for my brain damage. What's your excuse?"

She smiled gratefully. "I inherited it at birth."

"Celebration! To the kitchen everyone!" Mrs. Essig took two last pictures so that four of us were now rubbing our eyes. "There are cookies and powdered milk waiting."

Everyone groaned, and Dr. Essig bargained until Mrs. Essig agreed to open one of the last remaining liters of soda. We sat around the large pine picnic table in the kitchen, talking, swallowing down Oreos and draining the pop with relish. I'm not sure how we got onto the subject of traveling, but we did, and the morning took a sudden turn toward disaster.

Cristy began explaining that since the age of twelve she'd been planning a trip to New York with her cousin, Deborah. It was to be a graduation gift from Mr. and Mrs. Essig and the dream of a lifetime. She brought it up when we were on the last few drops of soda, after we'd emptied two packages of cookies. She asked us if we thought she should allocate some of her savings for a new camera, or if she should just keep it to spend when she arrived in New York.

Dr. Essig's answer was like a cardiac arrest.

"I'm sorry, honey," he began. "Your mother and I have been doing some serious thinking about your plans, and we've decided that you shouldn't go."

Cristy paled.

It was such a total surprise that even Edon appeared momentarily sympathetic.

"Yes, I know it's going to be a deep disappointment for you, but we see no alternative. New York is simply too dangerous to visit alone these days."

Cristy swallowed, trying to maintain self-control. "I don't believe you're doing this to me. You're teasing, right?" She turned to Mrs. Essig. "This is all a practical joke, isn't it?"

"No, dear, it isn't."

Cristy shot to her feet, her voice high and on the verge of hysteria. "You can't do this to me! You already said I could go. It was decided a long time ago!"

"We never gave our final permission, Cristy," Dr. Essig reminded her. "You just assumed we'd say yes."

"And, besides, that was before the accident," Mrs. Essig added quietly.

"The accident!" Cristy blinked back tears. "How long are we going to suffer for *the accident*!"

"We all have to be careful now." Dr. Essig pushed himself away from the table and faced her.

"Careful! You're not careful. You're schizoid!"

"Don't get smart, young lady!" It was a bellow from deep inside his chest.

"It's true! Wayne is gone, and there's nothing we can do about it! We can't live in a box forever, Dad. You can't treat me like this just because you're scared."

"Cut it out, Cris." Edon's heart was pounding through her T-shirt.

"Don't you dare tell me what to do!" Cristy shot back, glaring. "You baby them as much as they baby us. Everybody's getting worse instead of better. Wayne would be disgusted with all of us."

"What always makes you think you know what Wayne would be thinking!" Edon shouted. "You don't know!"

Dr. Essig pounded his fist on the table so that the dishes rattled. One slid off and shattered against the floor. Melissa started to sob. "I want each of us to calm down!" he roared.

"Calm down? *Calm down?*" Cristy stared at him. "I'm getting out of here!" She shoved a chair out of her way and stomped from the room. Seconds passed, the front door slammed, and suddenly it was very quiet.

Mrs. Essig reached for Melissa and cradled her in her arms.

Edon stood to pat her father's arm. "Don't worry, Dad. Cristy just needs to cool off by herself. It'll be okay in a few hours. She'll probably even apologize."

"I don't want an apology," Dr. Essig said, rubbing the temples of his forehead with his index fingers. "I want things to get back to normal again."

"They can't. It won't ever be the way it was, Eric. Too much has happened." Mrs. Essig's chin was quivering.

"We can be a family, Martha. We *will* be a family minus one. I'm not giving up until we are!"

A few minutes later I was sitting alone in the kitchen. It had happened again. The Swiss Family Robinson had just exploded. I was beginning to resent these scenes as much as Edon. I wanted to shout, too. I wanted to yell at Dr. Essig and tell him he was being unfairly restrictive, and that if he didn't relax, he was going to drive everyone nuts. I wanted to tell Cristy to be more patient and to stop her outbursts. She was acting like a child—also making everyone crazy.

But I kept still.

At times like these, when I felt like an outsider, I went to my balloon. It was the only connection I had with my own home and family. I was surprised to find Cristy there, leaning against the inside edge. I immediately thought about the money, which I had stuck back into the champagne bottle for safekeeping. But her face was as grim now as when she'd stormed out of the house, so I knew she hadn't found anything.

"Hi," I said, forcing her chin to come off her chest to look at me.

"Oh." She started. "Hi. I hope you don't mind me standing in your basket."

"No. I don't care." I grabbed a bar and hopped in beside her. "I plan on taking Edon up one of these days. You're welcome to come with us if you like."

"Oh, I'd love it!" she exclaimed, her face brightening for a few seconds. Her scowl quickly returned. "But I'm sure my parents wouldn't let me. Ed either. They'd say it was too dangerous."

"Maybe not." I glanced upward at the cloudless sky. "It's not always going to be like it is right now, you know."

Cristy stared at me, disagreement sparking like a dynamite fuse in her round blue eyes. "It's been almost a year since Wayne's accident, and they're worse today than they were then."

"A year." I gave an exaggerated shrug. "And what's supposed to happen in a year? You think they should've forgotten him completely by now?"

"No." She seemed surprised that I would say such a calloused thing. But that's exactly how she sounded when she forced her parents with the subject. "Of course not. But you don't understand how restrictive they've been since it happened. I can't breathe."

"Yeah. That's what you keep telling everyone."

"You think I'm selfish, don't you?"

I hadn't thought about it, but now that she'd mentioned the word, it kind of fit. "Yes. In a way I guess I do. Your parents really knock themselves out for you, and although they're overprotective, I would never judge them to be as horrible as you make them sound."

"Oh, you wouldn't, would you!" She glared at me. "Well, I think they need professional help. I think there's something wrong with them, and they're not going to get better on their own."

"They lost their son." A mournfulness swelled inside me when I said the words. "It's harder for them to recover than it is for you, or Edon, or Melissa. That's just the way it goes. If you give them some time, they'll probably change their mind about New York."

"How much time? A decade or two?"

"I'd say only a few more months."

"Do you really think so?"

"I'd bet my balloon on it."

"But I still feel they're upset beyond what's normal about Wayne. Especially Dad. I think there's something more to it with him." She pushed her blond hair away from her face and cocked her head to study me. "Were you suspicious when you discovered that the owner's plaque was missing from the panel here?" She pointed to the empty square.

"I knew it had probably been removed. Maybe I sent it to be engraved before I left."

"Or maybe someone took it off after you landed."

My heart began to pound within me. "What are you driving at, Cristy?"

"I don't know. I just think it's strange that your plaque was missing. No one could find any ID, and Dad isn't locating anyone who's looking for you. It's been weeks since your family saw you last. Surely that would frighten them enough to file a missing person report. Plus, you disappeared in a balloon. That's pretty conspicuous, don't you think?" She didn't allow me time to answer.

"Edon told me that balloonists have a ground crew that chases them during a flight, to help pick up the balloon and basket when it lands. Why haven't *they* reported anything?"

I blinked dumbly.

It's hard to admit that you're not indispensable, and that no one is frantic to find you—not your parents, not your chase crew, not even the police. It goes beyond the word unpopular to more like tragic. "There's probably a good reason for it. I just don't know what it is."

"How about someone might be trying to find you, but my parents aren't telling you about it?"

I shook my head in double time. "Don't be ridiculous, Cristy. Just because your parents are restrictive is no reason to accuse them of kidnapping. They're not the type."

"They *weren't* the type." Her shapely lips drew together in a pout. "But now I don't know. They're so possessive that I'm not sure what they would or wouldn't do. They've cheered up so much since you came here. They love taking care of you, and maybe they're just not ready to let you go."

"I don't think so, Cristy." I wished I could've sounded more confident. But Dr. Essig was, in fact, desperate. Under pressure to get his family back to normal again, he might be capable... I hated myself for even considering it.

"Okay, fine. If it doesn't bother you, it doesn't bother me. I just thought I should say something." She smiled, trying to make the atmosphere less tense. "Actually, I'm glad you're still here, too. This place would've been too dismal to survive if it hadn't been for you."

"Oh, sure. People with only half of a face, and even less of a brain, are always great company."

"No. I mean it. I bet you have a fiancé waiting for you somewhere, too."

"Come on. I'm too young to have a fiancé." I laughed nervously.

"I don't think so." She paused. "I'd say you're even old enough to have a wife."

I choked. Edon and Cristy sure had different opinions about things. "I'm pretty positive I'm not married."

"But you're very mature," she persisted. "And extremely knowledgeable about things. I think it's sweet the way you're always letting Ed tag along with you, too."

"I like her company."

"She's so young, though. A child compared to you."

"I don't feel that way. Edon's a smart girl."

"But she is *just* a girl. And you," she said, leveling her powder-blue gaze. "You're almost a man."

Cristy definitely had a way about her.

She'd been watching too many romance movies, though. There was no way any person with twenty-twenty vision would call me a man, as in earn-enough-money-to-support-a-family man. A guy with enough take-home pay for an out-to-dinner spot a couple of times a month maybe.

But no dependents.

She certainly was cute, though. And the way she kept blinking those mirrors to her heart and giving me little crooked smiles, I knew she wanted to kiss me.

It was tempting. Cristy was pretty enough to claim universal beauty titles. But I was reluctant. It didn't feel right.

I let the moment slip away.

"Excuse me. Dad wants to talk to you." Edon's voice was flat, like a robot who'd never had any tone programmed into it.

Cristy abruptly stepped back, her manner full of guilt. "Can't I have any time to myself? Is there some unwritten law somewhere that commands you to bother me?"

"Dad's the one who wants you. Not me."

"Why didn't he come and get me himself?"

"I don't know. Why don't you go and ask him? Actually, it's just as well that it was me who walked up instead of Dad, don't you think?"

Cristy climbed out of the basket. "I'm not going to back down this time. I'm telling Dad straight."

"Uh, excuse me, Cristy, but what were you doing before? Humbly submitting?"

"It's going to have to change. I'm not spending the prime of my life in a closet."

"Excuse me again, Cristy, but didn't you say the prime of your life was last summer? I mean, is this going to be an everlasting prime, or will it peak out when you're fifty or sixty or so?"

Cristy brushed by her sister, her chin up as though she were strolling through neck-deep water. "At your age, I don't expect you to understand." She hesitated when she reached the edge of the cabin. "Thanks for talking with me, Mason. You're about the only person around here who still has his wits about him."

"Oh, right," Edon said, once Cristy was gone. "A guy who doesn't know his own name has his wits about him."

"Hey. There's no need to be hostile."

She scoffed. "The only reason she likes you now is because your face is fixed. You weren't worth her time when your nose was broken."

"She can't help it if she's unable to tolerate the sight of wounded people."

"She doesn't think of anyone but herself."

"It's hard being seventeen."

"And it's smooth as ice cream living out fourteen? Give me a break, Mason. If you want to fall in love with Cristy, go for it. But at least have the decency not to sneak around behind everyone's back. Good grief! Dad probably saved your life."

"That's right, Edon. Your dad saved my life, opened his home to me, nursed me to health, and now I'm putting the moves on his daughter. Cristy's just my type, too. A real reasonable, even-tempered girl."

"With her looks she doesn't have to be reasonable." She whisked a tall blade of grass from the ground and began winding it between her fingers. "So do you love her or not?"

"Has anyone ever told you you were too shy?"

"Never."

"Have you ever wondered why?" I heaved a deep sigh. "Look, everyone in your family is upset right now. It's very tense around here."

"You think I don't know it?"

"It's not the time for me to be searching for a mate. I just wanted to see peace for more than forty-eight hours at a shot. Your sister felt like talking, and I thought it might help if someone listened."

"Help? Who? Cristy?" Edon threw her now mutilated sliver of grass to the ground. "She doesn't need help. She needs a kick in the rump. She's behaving like a spoiled child, and Mom and Dad have enough troubles without her spouting off stupid threats whenever she doesn't get her way!''

"Edon," I said softly, hoping to calm her down. "I want to help your parents, too. I like all of you. I really hate seeing everyone so unhappy.''

She gazed at me, her eyes filling with tears. "It's all because of Wayne, you know.''

"I know.''

"If he hadn't bought that stupid bike, he'd still be—'' She turned away. "Oh, Mason, do you think we'll ever be a normal family again? The way Dad wants us to be?''

Swinging my legs over the edge of the basket, I landed beside her and lifted her chin so she would see me more directly. I wanted no mistake in her understanding my sincerity. "You know you will. Your family is trying too hard to make it happen for it not to. It just takes time.''

"But everyone's so emotional.''

"Time.''

"And Cristy never compromises.''

"Time.''

"Do you always have to repeat yourself?''

"Only when I'm with you.''

She wiped the tears off her cheeks and gave a weak grin. "You sound so confident about it. As though you really believe it will happen.''

"I honestly figure it will." I put my arm around her and led her slowly toward the cabin. I was trying to think of something to do to get her mind off things. "Hey! We could help the situation a little right now if you like.''

"How?"

"We could make dinner tonight. I'm sure your mom is going to be tired after all this, and Cristy and your dad need to talk things out. We could make spaghetti, rolls, and open a can of pinto beans."

"Beans, Mason?" Edon rolled her eyes. "With spaghetti?"

"Okay, then. A can of hominy."

"Gag me."

"Limas?"

She stuck out the tip of her tongue.

"Fine. You choose the vegetable."

"Peas."

"Wonderful. Spaghetti, rolls, peas and powdered milk."

"We'll put chocolate in it to make it taste better."

"What? The spaghetti?"

"Forget it, Mason." She giggled. "What would we do without you?"

Chapter Four

Isn't it strange that when a person tells you absolutely not to do something, that's absolutely what you do? You're sitting in the cafeteria and someone starts talking about someone else who's walking by. They keep adding "don't look" every few words, but man, it's as if there's a magnet stuck to the side of your face. You can't fight this overwhelming sensation to move your vision to the target. Your friend ends up thoroughly disgusted with you. "Didn't I say *not to look*?" he growls, before he asks you if you understand English. His face turns red, and you spend the next five minutes assuring him that the girl didn't know what he was saying.

Here's another one. "Don't stay out too late." Same thing happens. A giant magnet damages the accuracy of your digital watch so that you never return home before ten o'clock on a week night.

And then there's the hundreds of "don'ts" you received while you were growing up. The first, a sorry joke from parents to toddlers, "Now don't put that oatmeal on your head!" Others to follow were: "Don't touch the light socket," "Don't fall in the water," "Don't hit the ball toward the window," "Don't touch the cake," "Don't forget to zip your pants," and "Don't ask for the car keys."

These warnings were common knowledge, as obvious as the facts that people need air and birds like worms. I couldn't remember the situations, but I knew they'd happened. And just to be consistent, when I told myself not to think about Cristy's accusation that her parents were maneuvering things to keep me from my real home, that's exactly what I did think about.

Again and again. More disturbing than that, her words were sounding possible.

Eighty-five percent of me thought the Essigs were innocent, and yet it was that little bit of doubt that was changing my entire outlook on things.

If there was even the slightest chance that Dr. Essig was withholding information from me, I couldn't stay with them. I was going to have to move out and try to find my real home on my own.

What a mess. Here I was, sure that the Essigs were the most loving and trusting people in the world, and yet I couldn't live with them anymore. I had Cristy to thank for it, too. I'd tried to change her opinion of her parents and, instead, she'd changed mine. Her attitude was improving some, though. During our final weeks at the cabin, her outbursts were fewer, although her stubbornness continued as firm as concrete.

It really helped me to appreciate Edon. She'd begun to avoid most of the family confrontations. I could tell there were times when she wanted to strangle Cristy, but she kept her mouth shut. Another loud voice would only inch the problem out of control again. And Edon was smart enough to know it.

She was also the best kind of friend a guy could want. It was difficult for me to tell her I wouldn't be staying around when we got to Phoenix. I expected that she would be unhappy with my decision, but I didn't think it would bother her as much as it did.

"But why?" she gasped, her green eyes filling with disappointment. I'd asked her to take a walk along the creek so no one would hear if her temper erupted.

"I just think it's best."

"Oh, you do, do you!" She grabbed a rock and sent it skittering across the surface of the water. Edon had a great sidearm. Dr. Essig had told me she played shortstop in her P.E. class all the time. "When did you decide to start giving your own diagnosis?"

"I'm not a patient anymore, Edon. My head is healed."

"Not the inside." She pinned one hand to her waist and used the other to shake her finger at me. "As long as you have amnesia, you're still sick and should remain under medical supervision. You just can't go wandering off whenever the mood suits you. You're not the doctor."

I leaned against the base of a young pine tree and folded my arms across my chest trying to look posed when, actually, I was thinking hard. Edon had brought up a point I hadn't considered.

I was still Dr. Essig's patient. Technically I was ill. He wouldn't allow me to leave his care if he thought I wasn't fully recovered.

"Edon," I began with authority. "I have the final say as to when I go or come. It could be another six months, maybe more, before my memory returns. I'm going to have to start living my life again."

"Excuuuuse me, Mason. I thought you were living a life here. With us."

"I was. I mean, I am. But I've got to do something to find my family."

"But Daddy *is* trying to find your family." Her voice softened. "Why don't you just leave it up to him? He knows what he's doing. How could you uncover more information than him?"

"I don't know." I coughed nervously. "Maybe it's just something I've got to do. Maybe I don't feel it's right to sit around and let everyone else do stuff that's my responsibility."

"But it never bothered you to let him do it before." She straightened suddenly, her eyes narrowing suspiciously. "I know what's really wrong!"

I clamped my lips together, promising myself I wouldn't confess Cristy's accusation no matter how close Edon came to guessing it.

"You're tired of us!" she sputtered.

"What?"

"You think we're too messed up to help, and so it's goodbye baby, so long loony birds."

"Are you crazy?"

"I know your type, Mason. Float in on an unsuspecting family, make them love you and then hit the road Jack. Cold turkey. Mean meat."

I grinned at her. "You guys love me?"

She blinked, her cheeks flushing pink beneath her tan. "Of course. What do you think?"

Her words made me feel wonderful. With all the insecurities of not knowing where you come from, having someone to love you is as important as food to eat and water to drink.

"But I see Mr. Mason Redford from Moscow can live with people an entire summer and not feel any responsibility or kinship toward them."

"That's not true, Edon." I could tell I'd hurt her. Still, if I were completely honest about my reasons for leaving, it would only make matters worse. "I'm not going because I want to. You have to understand that. I'm going because I *have* to."

"That doesn't make sense. You have a home with us."

"Yes, but don't you see, Edon? It's not the home I came from. I have a responsibility to my real family, too."

"Daddy's looking for them. You can't do any more than he's doing."

"I have to try, Edon. Especially now. Whether I want to or not, I've got to try for myself." I reached out to touch her hand.

"What about money? You need money to live on," she said.

"There was some in the basket."

"It can't be enough to last for very long."

"Sure it can."

"You'll have to get a job, and then you won't be able to go to school."

"Yes, I will."

"And what kind of a place could you afford? You don't want to live in the slums where the train hobos stay."

"I won't."

"And you have to eat."

"You bet."

"I mean you really eat, Mason, and that costs money."

"I've got enough."

"I'm not going to lend you any either because I don't agree with what you're doing."

"I understand."

She shot another rock into the water. "Maybe a hundred or so, but don't ask for more."

"I won't need any."

She glanced at me curiously. "Exactly how much money do you have, Mason?"

I pushed a pocket of air back and forth from one cheek to the other. If there was a person anywhere in the western hemisphere I could trust, it was Edon. I needed to relieve guilt like a train needed to release steam. I'd been holding too much back. I was desperate to have someone to confide in.

I sucked in my breath ready to give it a try. "It has to remain confidential between the two of us."

"All right."

"It can't go any farther than this creek."

"It won't."

"You have to give me your word."

"My word."

"I mean, nothing to nobody."

"All right, already, Mason! What do you want me to do? Cut off my finger and sign a contract?"

I exhaled loudly. "A hundred thousand dollars."

She stared at me. "You're joking."

"Nope."

"You're trying to impress me."

"I'm impressive enough. It's the truth."

"A hundred thousand dollars?"

I nodded.

"Where did you get it, Mason? No one carries around a hundred thousand dollars! Not the pope, not TV evangelists. Not even the president!"

"I know that, Edon. I don't understand it all either."

"Are you Arabic?"

"Blondes aren't usually from Arabia."

"But you're filthy rich anyway?"

"All I have is the hundred thousand dollars. And it wasn't mine to begin with. I sort of inherited it."

I explained about the champagne bottle and told her exactly what was written on the note. She said she admired the writer's sense of values but was pretty positive she couldn't hand a twenty-dollar bill away, let alone a tenth of a million dollars. She also wondered if the owner of the champagne bottle knew whose balloon it was. She thought there might be a possibility that someone specifically wanted it to be me who found the money.

"But why wouldn't they have just handed it over in person?" I asked.

"Maybe they wanted you to think about their message more. I mean, this is really a dramatic way to make a point, don't you think?"

"You're right," I admitted, all sorts of possibilities beginning to whiz through my head. "Maybe someone on my chase crew put it there. Maybe I have a rich relative who wants me to grow up as a man with ethics."

Edon started to laugh. "'A man with ethics.' Sounds like a complicated movie with a bad ending."

"Oh, yeah?" I grabbed her, pretending to throw her into the creek. "You're just jealous because you don't have wealthy friends."

She clung to me like a cat, giggling and pleading until I finally released her. Suddenly her expression became serious.

"Mason," she said, "if you have wealthy friends, why haven't they been able to find you? Rich people should have all sorts of ways to locate a missing person."

"That's why I have to move out. There are a lot of questions I need to find the answers to."

"Yes, but you're not making any sense. How would moving out help you? It seems to me that it would only complicate your life. I can understand your wanting to start checking into things yourself, but you can do that from our house. What's the big deal?"

Edon was smart. Sometimes she was too smart.

"Maybe I'm beginning to feel like a burden. Maybe I feel as if I've overstayed my welcome."

"You know that's not true." Her eyes narrowed. "There's something you're not telling me, Mason. You've been acting funny for a couple of weeks now, and you'd probably feel a hundred percent better if you'd just tell me what it is.''

"You think so?"

"I'm sure of it.''

I shook my head. "Well, my lips are sealed. In fact, I think it's best we drop the subject."

Edon stepped back to face me more squarely. Bears would learn to fly before she would ever follow a suggestion. "Let me put things clearly, Mason. Dad's not going to let you go without a fight. And, in my opinion, he's absolutely right. He has good reasons for keeping you under surveillance. You still have amnesia and require medical assistance. He's put himself out on a limb keeping you at his home and observing symptoms instead of skipping you to an X-ray machine. He's assisted you through a difficult healing process, and if something should go wrong now, he'd hold himself personally responsible." Her look softened. "You have to trust Dad's judgment more, Mason. After all, he's a friend as much as he is your doctor."

It was almost funny. Cristy was trying to convince me to watch out for Dr. Essig, that he might not be plugged in upstairs, and Edon was telling me to trust him more, that he was my friend as well as my doctor.

"Have I ever asked you for a favor?" she questioned, her voice tender.

"No-o-o," I replied cautiously.

"If I asked you to do something that was very important to me, do you think you would?"

"Probably."

"It would really hurt Dad's feelings if you disregarded his professional opinion in this case. He's grown extremely fond of you. Can you understand that?''

It was my turn to send a rock skittering across the creek. "I guess."

"Please, Mason, as a favor to me, could you stay with us for just a while longer?" She hesitated. "Please?"

It was all over. I'd have felt like the biggest pile of slime ever if I'd said no. She looked so earnest, and so serious. So worried. "Okay, you win," I sighed. "But I'm going to start searching for my family on my own."

She reached up to give me a grateful hug. "That's fine, Mason. I'm sure Daddy would appreciate your help."

"Let's hope so," I said beneath my breath. "If not, we're all in trouble."

Phoenix. It seemed like a big cement mistake compared to the rainbow-colored peaks of the mountains. It was loud and congested and complex. I recognized it as I'd recognized the elms of the Canyon.

I'd lived here before.

It was exciting at first. At least now I knew what city I was from. Still, I didn't have any idea how I was supposed to penetrate it to find my home. There were thousands and thousands of people. Nearly as many buildings. I'd thought coming to Phoenix would make things easier, but I felt as if I'd stepped from a puzzle into a huge, hopeless maze. The aftershock was hard to take. I fell into my first deep depression. Doc said it was to be expected, but I was miserable. Nothing seemed to be important. The mornings were gray, the afternoons endless, and the nights made my stomach hurt.

Edon and Cristy invited their friends over, trying to get me involved in things. I liked Edon's crowd better than Cristy's, even though they were younger. Cristy had this one friend named Trixie who—I promise—looked like a snake. She was tall and skinny and had sneaky, slanted eyes packed with silver eye shadow. She kind of hissed when she talked, never said anything nice about anyone and, no joke, the only thing she was missing was fangs.

Edon's best friend, Julie, was shy and quiet and sort of cute. Except when she giggled, then the whole house shook. I'm not sure why she was so loud, but what she didn't say all day she made up for in one sixty-second laugh.

The rest of their friends were pretty normal. They seemed to accept me all right when I was around, which wasn't much. I spent most of the time in my room, staring at the sailboat I'd brought from the cabin, trying to get up enough courage to begin the search for my family. It seemed so hopeless.

Edon had been right. Getting my own place would've just complicated things. The Essig home was comfortable, upper middle class. It had a big lawn, citrus trees, flagstone patio and a pool in the back. It also had the Essigs themselves, and I had to admit, overcoming my depression would've been difficult without them.

They just wouldn't give up. I never saw so many smiles, or heard so many diagnoses of beautiful days in my life. Even more amazing, they stopped fighting.

They became so concerned with me that they quit worrying about their own problem. The peace was great. When I started to feel better, I toyed with the idea of faking it. I could pretend to be depressed for years, and I'd never have to hear another argument again. Dr. Essig would have his "normal" family back, Cristy could keep her new personality, and Edon would be happy.

Too bad I was such a bad actor. Edon noticed my mood change right away. She immediately began encouraging me to make the first step in finding out who I was. She said it would make me feel good, even if I wasn't instantly successful.

I believed her.

My heart was pounding like a machine gun when I picked up the receiver.

"Phoenix City Police, Information."

I cleared my throat. "I'd like to speak to someone about a missing person."

"One moment."

The knots in my stomach tightened as I listened to the clicks of the transfer.

"Officer Penners, Homicide."

"Homicide? Excuse me, I wanted Missing Persons."

"Same thing. May I help you?"

It wasn't the same thing in my mind at all. I wasn't dead. I was lost. "I want to find out if there was a missing person report filed on someone about two and a half months ago."

"Last name, please."

"Of who?"

"The missing person. I need it for the computer. Last name, please."

"Uh. I don't have it."

"I need the last name, or I can't locate the report."

"What about a physical description? I have a physical description."

He was quiet for a few seconds. "Did you find a stiff?"

"Excuse me?"

"A body. A dead person."

"No, sir."

"A golden oldie who doesn't have a resting place? Did you find a golden oldie?"

"What's a golden oldie?"

"A senior citizen who can't remember where he came from."

"No, sir. All I have is the physical description of someone who I'm pretty sure was reported missing two and a half months ago."

"But you don't know his name?"

"That's right."

It was quiet again. "Okay, bud. Let's hear what you have."

"Blond, male, white, six feet, blue eyes, a hundred and fifty-five pounds. Lost in the state of Arizona."

"Age?"

"Seventeen to twenty."

"Give me a break!"

"Sir?"

I could hear him tapping something. A pencil, a pen. His gun. "Okay. I'll be honest with you. If I pulled all the names that fit that description from the computers I'd probably end up with thirty different people. It would be a big time-consuming mess. It would take weeks, maybe months to check it all out." He sounded bored. The tapping slowed. "Now, if you want to tell me who you are, what you found, and why you're asking about this person, I might be persuaded to invest some additional time."

For a minute I considered throwing myself at the mercy of Officer Penners. However, he didn't seem accustomed to having lost people hunt for themselves and was too suspicious of me. I thought about the one hundred thousand dollars and how incriminating that might look to a homicide investigator. I also wondered if Dr. Essig might be in any trouble if it was discovered that he'd been withholding information.

Thirty people wasn't exactly pinpointing my identity anyway.

I decided to go it alone for a while longer. "Thanks anyway, sir, but I think I'll try something else."

"Suit yourself." He said something about "world full of mistakes" before the receiver clicked to a buzz in my ear.

I walked into the kitchen, my mind working over what he'd told me. Thirty missing people reports that fit my physical description. I took three Popsicles from the freezer, went to the back porch and stared at the pool.

Thirty missing people reports, and Dr. Essig hadn't said a word.

Chapter Five

Dr. Essig was sitting at the head of the table. Mrs. Essig was at the opposite end. Cristy and Edon took up one side, and Melissa and I sat at the other. A colorful flower arrangement was centered on the long oak table. The chandelier above was dimmed appropriately, and we all had cloth napkins across our laps. Dinner had become much more formal in Phoenix, with full seven-course meals and crystal water glasses.

The Essigs were once again the perfect family unit. Especially now that the hard-core arguing had stopped. A nice, perfect mother, two pretty, perfect daughters, a perfect little girl... There was only one problem.

The perfect father was a kidnapper.

I stared at him out of the corner of my eye. I watched everything he did. I watched how he bit into the chicken. I watched how his mustache wiggled around when he chewed. I timed how long he took to swallow and make his Adam's apple bulge and retreat.

Bulge and retreat. Bulge and retreat. I'd glance down whenever he looked up so he wouldn't know. Why did you lie, Doc? Bulge and retreat. Don't you feel guilty about keeping me from my family? Bulge and retreat. Do you think that just because you saved my life you own it, too? Bulge and retreat. How about a confession? How about you tell me the facts and I won't have you thrown in jail? How about a little truth serum? How about—

"Would you like more mashed potatoes, Mason?" Mrs. Essig held the pink china bowl in the air.

"Uh, no thanks."

Edon was staring at me. She'd been watching me watch her dad. I slid my plate away.

"May I be excused?" Everyone looked at me as though I'd said something amazing.

"But, Mason, you didn't even touch your chicken!" Mrs. Essig gave her husband an "I'm worried about him so why don't you do something" look.

Bulge and retreat. "Mason, ol' man, don't you feel up to par this evening?"

"No, sir, I don't."

"Is it something specific? Your stomach?"

I shook my head.

"Do you have a headache?"

"No. I just don't feel much like eating. I think I'd like to lie down awhile. Nothing to worry about." I shrugged. "Really. It's okay."

I was behaving too peculiarly. I could see it in everyone's expression. "Maybe it *is* my stomach. I ate about four million Popsicles today. I'll take some antacid tablets."

Dr. Essig started to get up. "Here, I'll find something for you."

"No, no." *No kidnappers in my room please.* "I'll get some Alka-Seltzer. It'll be fine. Really." I left quickly before anyone could say anything else.

I closed my door, locked it and dug the champagne bottle out from behind some books in the wall unit. There were lots of books in my room, which was really a guest room, den and study combined. They hadn't offered Wayne's room. I wouldn't have taken it if they had. Not with me suspecting the doc the way I was.

Wayne's room was like a shrine. Everything had been kept the way it was when he died. His favorite posters were on the wall, his schoolbooks were stacked neatly on his desk, and a few dirt-biking trophies lined a shelf, along with a baseball mitt and separate pictures of Edon, Cristy, Melissa, and the doc and Mrs. Essig together. The only thing that had really changed was his closet, which was now completely empty. The Essigs tried to act as if it were just another room now, and as soon as they had time, they would gather up all the textbooks, trophies, posters and pictures, put them all away and make good use of the room.

It was a facade, of course. Letting go of that room meant letting go of Wayne. Maybe they were afraid they would forget him. But I knew that would never happen. People don't forget people when they die. They can't, even if they try.

I carefully pulled the cork out. I'd hidden the bottle behind the books because I was afraid Mrs. Essig might find it in my drawer. I didn't think she was the type to rummage through my things, but she might accidentally run across it when she was putting away clothes or tidying up. Even hiding it under the bed or in the closet seemed risky.

I unpeeled a five-thousand-dollar bill and the note. I planned to cash in five thousand at a bank tomorrow. I wanted to pay the Essigs for the clothes they'd bought me and for all the food they'd given me. I'd already explained that I'd found some extra money tucked in the console when I was checking the gondola for damage. They wouldn't be suspicious as long as I didn't go overboard. Suddenly, it was very important to me not to take favors. Paying the Essigs was, in a way, like staying loyal to my own family.

My own family. I didn't want to think about it. There was this acidic uneasiness in the pit of my belly whenever I tried to remember anything. I'd force my mind blank and then strain my brain. It was as though I were taking an incredibly intense geometry test and I'd keep commanding myself to concentrate, concentrate, concentrate. Nothing would happen. *Concentrate, concentrate, concentrate.* Blackness. My voice would begin screaming inside my head. *Concentrate! Remember your family! Remember your family!* Then the acid sickness would begin to seep into my belly. I couldn't keep the Essigs from infiltrating my thoughts. My brain would begin pounding. Then I'd give up.

I never daydreamed of what my mother might look like or what kind of man my father was. I never tried to imagine myself with brothers or sisters. It had become too frustrating. Too emotional. Too sad.

It was my conscience that was making me face up to things. As a living, breathing son to someone, I had to find my parents. It was my duty. Pounding brain, acid sickness, frustration. My conscience wouldn't let anything stop me anymore.

Uncurling the note to lay flat on the desk, I stared at it. What a crummy clue. It wasn't even handwritten. There weren't any typing errors or spelling mistakes. No letterhead. The only thing I could conclude was that it was written by an adult, a front-page revelation since kids don't usually have a hundred thousand dollars lying around to give away.

Whoever it was did have ideals, though.

"Money is a poor substitute for love," I said aloud. "Wealth was meant to be shared. If not, you have nothing, and you are indeed a poor man."

Wow.

There was a loud rapping on the door. I jumped and nearly busted my head on the overhead lamp. Too bad. If I'd connected right, it might have knocked my memory back. I stuffed the note, the money and the bottle under the desk in the far corner.

"Come in."

"I can't. The door's locked." Edon's voice was hushed.

I opened the door for her. "Okay, Mason, what's going on," she demanded, tromping across the floor and flopping on my bed.

"Make yourself comfortable." I rubbed my face, fingering the stiff, dark hairs that lately had been multiplying into a follicle forest above my lip and across my chin. "Do you think this growth warrants an investment in a razor? Or maybe I should keep it for the laid-back look."

"Don't try to change the subject. Why are you acting so weird?"

"I'm not." I put my hand over my stomach. "I told you earlier, I ate too many Popsicles."

"Why were you looking at Dad so much. Don't you think he has manners?"

"He has great manners, just like the rest of you, minus Melissa."

"Why was the door locked?"

"I had to see the note again, and I didn't want anyone to walk in, okay?"

She relaxed and took on a look of guilt. "Sorry. The way you were watching Dad ... I don't know. I just thought ..." She stood up. "Julie and I are going to see a movie. I thought you might like to come."

"When?"

"In about an hour."

"I'll see how I feel."

I decided to go. It was good to get out of the house. Ever since I'd had the telephone conversation with Officer Penners, I'd felt boxed in. Claustrophobic. The theater we were going to was located in a mall, and Edon and Julie had arranged it so we would have time to do some shopping before the film started. It was entertaining the way they teased each other back and forth. Julie's laugh would ring down the mall whenever Edon said something funny.

"Julie's always having some kind of ridiculous dream that she needs my help with," Edon was explaining. "Like when we first met, she kept dreaming that this giant frog would glue his sticky tongue against her and then flop her back and forth between two lily pads.''

"It was awful." Julie bounced her head between her hands. "I felt like a yo-yo. I'd get moss all over me, fish in my mouth and my perm would come out."

"Sounds awful. How did you ever cure her of it, Edon?"

"I told her to stop sleeping in her aquarium."

They burst out laughing, and the people in front of us turned around to see what was going on.

"Rib-splitting," I replied, realizing that I couldn't remember ever having a dream. I wondered if people with amnesia were capable of dreaming.

Edon stopped suddenly. She grabbed my hand and pulled me through a stream of people to the opposite side of the mall. "See," she said, pointing to a mannequin in a window. "What do you think? Do you like it?"

I guessed that she was talking about the baby blue dress the mannequin was wearing. "It looks feminine enough for Cristy, but I think she might like a blouse better. Unless it's for your mom. It might be a little young for your mom, though."

"I'm not talking about buying it for Cristy or Mom. I'm talking about buying it for me."

"For you? But, Edon, it's a dress."

Julie started laughing, and a baby in a stroller woke up crying. "I know. I couldn't believe it either. Ed always wears pants."

"So maybe I want to expand my horizons some. There's nothing wrong with that." She waved Julie off. "What do you think, Mason Redford?"

"It's pastel blue, Edon."

"Yes. I know my colors, Mason."

"Well, I'm used to seeing you in army green."

"You don't think I'd look good in it, do you?"

"I never said that." I took her by the shoulders and moved her against the glass beside the mannequin. Putting my thumb up like an artist, I shut one eye and focused first on the dress, then on Edon, then on the dress again, then back on Edon. Julie shook with giggles.

"Hurry up, Mason! The movie's going to start." Edon shifted her weight uneasily. "Anyway, it's not nice to gape at a person!"

"I'm not gaping. I want to give you a thorough, responsible answer." I kept my gaze the same, until finally, she pushed herself away from the glass.

"Good grief, Mason! If it's that hard, just forget it."

I sighed very deeply. "I just wanted to do a good job, Edon."

"Forget it. Forget I even said anything."

"But I tried so hard. Don't you want to hear my conclusion?"

"No."

"Oh, Ed, don't be a baby. Come on, Mason. Tell us what you think!" Julie attempted to be serious. I cleared my throat importantly.

"I think that frilly, baby-blue dress would look absolutely and wholly awesome on you, Edon."

Her face lit up as if someone had just handed her twenty credit cards. "Really? Awesome?"

"Pretty, too. And if you would allow me the honor, I'd like to buy it for you."

Julie looked astonished. "Hey, I have a few things I want to ask your opinion on, too, Mason. They're in the jewelry store. Fourteen-karat section."

"Do you really think you should?" Forty bucks to a guy with a hundred thousand dollars was like one egg in a bucket of caviar. Edon smiled. "It's very thoughtful of you, Mason Redford from Moscow, and I accept."

The movie was about a man wrongly accused of murder. He had only twenty-four hours to come up with the real assailant, or be subject to a biased jury that was sure to find him guilty as charged, a plucked jailbird to go. This guy really had to be clever with his clues, too. They were few and bleak. At one point he went to the local radio and television stations to see if they could recall any information on a past news story. He also checked the old newspapers in a library for any related articles.

Edon looked at me, and I knew we were thinking the same thing.

Surely someone would remember a report on a missing balloon! It was the kind of original material that journalists loved. So what if no one had heard anything while we were at the Grand Canyon. Maybe they'd just missed it. *Or had Dr. Essig kept it quiet?* The local television newswriters could probably recall it, or a disc jockey might remember reading it.

I'd found a new lead!

"Are you going to call some stations?" Edon whispered.

"Tomorrow." I handed her my carton of popcorn. It was impossible to concentrate on the movie anymore. The new lead, and how I was going to begin, was the main feature now.

The receiver felt slippery against my sweaty palm. The thought of finding my parents had caused a surge of nervousness inside me.

"Hello. KAPG. Big Bob Bowers here."

"Uh, hello. May I speak to the person who reads the news?"

"She's not here right now. May I help you?" His voice was full, flawless and unnaturally buoyant. I figured disc jockeys began talking that way at the age of three. It probably drove their mothers crazy, sounding so bouncy when they asked for their cereal in the morning.

"It's about a news report. You would have heard of it approximately two and a half months ago." My voice was beginning to grow deep and bouncy like his.

"Big Bob Bowers needs more details."

"It was about a missing guy in a missing hot air balloon." Was that really me?

"Up, up and away, huh? Big Bob Bowers doesn't have time for jokes."

"No, wait, really! A guy was honestly lost in a balloon. He disappeared early this summer." My voice was back to normal again. It sounded too high.

"Big Bob Bowers wouldn't forget something like that. I don't believe the story came through this station. Would you like to make a request?"

"No. No thanks."

"How about 'Somewhere Over the Rainbow'?" He chuckled.

"'My Home Town.' That sounds good."

"You got it, Balloon Man. And, remember, it was yours first at KAPG!"

On to the next station.

"Howdeeee. KBEE, the country sound without the city noise."

"Hello. I need to speak to your news department."

"I'm it. What can I do for you?"

"Do you recall reading a news report about two and a half months ago about a missing man in a missing hot air balloon?"

"Is this legit, son?"

"Yes, sir. We know for a fact that it happened. We just don't know if it was reported here in Phoenix."

"I get a news printout from a local television station. I don't write or research any of the stuff. I just put it on the air."

"Do you remember reading the report?"

"Nope. Sorry. Did they ever find the cowboy?"

"Sort of."

"You mean he was dead? Bouncin' beans, that's a hard way to go! Anything else, son?"

"No, sir. Thank you."

Onward.

"KDKD. What's your name?"

"Mason."

"Congratulations, Mason. You're our sixth caller! Okay, are you ready?"

"For what?"

"Just say stop when you hear the moo for you!"

A series of sounds like bawling cows echoed in my ear. I said stop at the fourth one. Bells started ringing, horns started blowing and people started clapping. The disc jockey finally cut the tape and came back on. "All right, Mason. Are you excited?"

"I'm confused."

He laughed. "Me, too, Mason. All the time. Okay, listen carefully for the prize selected from this moo's for you!"

Another tape came on, and a voice said, "Congratulations! You've just won the pet of your choice from Puppies and Things, the complete pet supply store for puppies, guppies and more. Located at 1212 East Broadway. Open everyday, nine to five." It clicked off.

"Well, what do you think, Mason?"

"I'm not sure."

"Who's the best station in town?"

"Is this KDKD?"

"That's right, Mason! You're not confused anymore! KDKD for all your rock and roll needs. The station with a moo for you!"

I wanted to take a break around two o'clock, but there was only one more number on the page, so I put a quarter in the slot and dialed it.

"KWWZ. Easy listening. William Keizer speaking."

"Hello. May I talk to the person who reads the news?"

"There are several. I do it Monday through Wednesday. Betty Franklin does it Thursday through Saturday. And we tape it for Sunday." He sounded in a hurry.

"I was wondering if you've read a report about a guy missing in a balloon?"

"Listen, bud, why don't you call KAPG? They like prank calls."

He hung up, and the quarter clunked into the pit of the phone. It sounded full. I'd spent the last four hours talking to radio stations. I hadn't talked constantly, since I'd let other people use the booth in between calls, but it was enough to make me hate pay telephones.

It hadn't helped either. After speaking with innumerable disc jockeys and newscasters—I'd dialed three numbers incorrectly, and the phone had eaten a quarter—and after guessing who was the seventh president, picking the moo for me, making seven requests and ordering five radio bumper stickers, I was face-to-face with a dead end. No one remembered anything about a missing balloon, but everyone was sure they would have if it had come through their station.

I wished I could recall something on my own. It was so frustrating never knowing. Never being sure. I was always up in the air about almost everything.

It wasn't easy staying cheerful under such conditions. A guy could end up on the verge of tears once a month or so, just from the stress of uncertainty, and that's not including the stress from disappointments, hopelessness and mental incompetence.

I was no exception, though I'd always keep times like those to myself.

Finding the nearest deli, I buried my failures in a meatball sub, potato salad and pickle lunch plate. I went to the bathroom to count out the money I would need to pay the waitress. I didn't want anyone to get suspicious about the remaining $4,990.43. She was probably going to faint at my five-dollar tip as it was.

The teller at the bank had acted very strangely when I'd requested to have the five-thousand-dollar bill cashed. A recent inheritance is how I'd explained it. He'd nodded politely, then excused himself with the bill and slipped into the back. I'd known they were probably checking to see if it was counterfeit. The possibility had crossed my mind, too. Maybe the guy who'd written the note wasn't as ethical as I'd thought. Maybe he was a clever crook with a sick sense of humor.

Waiting so long had made me nervous. But when the teller had returned, he'd apologized for the delay and had given me the bills and change I'd asked for. I had decided I'd hide most of them behind the curtain rod in my bedroom, taking down what I needed when I needed it.

When I left the deli, I took a cab to the mall and bought Edon the dress she liked. I also bought a nice pair of skates for Melissa, a clock radio for Cristy and a small portable television for the doc and Mrs. Essig.

Edon thought giving gifts was the best way to show my appreciation to the family, and I agreed it was safer than handing out cash. To pay them back for everything would be impossible, much too suspicious, so she suggested gifts. Gifts with prices that would be difficult to guess at. Edon thought they shouldn't total over a hundred dollars combined, either.

I'm afraid I slipped over her limit a bit....

I wasn't going to be stupid, though. After this, I would be careful about how much money I spent in front of the Essigs. And I'd start accepting the allowance that Dr. Essig kept trying to push on me. I would save it and return the entire sum to him when I found my family.

Chapter Six

The sun was just beginning to glide behind the mountaintops when I slipped through the front door. I could smell dinner cooking, so I knew everyone was either in the kitchen or watching TV in the living room. As quietly as possible, I moved the presents from the front porch to beneath everyone's chairs at the dining room table. Once, Melissa trotted through, and I had to cram myself and the TV into a corner where she couldn't see me.

I walked into the kitchen, very nonchalant. "Hi, Martha."

"Good grief, Mason, where have you been?" Mrs. Essig slammed a carrot on the counter before she turned to glare at me.

I swallowed. She'd never been mad at me before. "I've been running around. Shopping a little."

"Well, I've been worried sick! It's almost seven o'clock!"

"I guess I lost track of the time."

"I expect a phone call, young man. We're not running a hotel here." She looked as stern as a traffic cop.

We both just stared at each other. I didn't know what to say. I was in shock. The silence seemed to stretch into miles. Finally her look dropped, and she wiped her hands on the dish towel. I thought she was going to cry.

"I'm sorry, Mason. You must hate me for talking to you like that."

"No. It's my fault. It was thoughtless of me not to call."

"It's just that I worry. We're very fond of you."

"I'll call the next time."

She turned back to the counter, and when she picked up the carrot again, her fingers were trembling.

Melissa darted into the room. "Mason! Mason! We heard you on the radio today! What are you going to get? A horse? A puppy? Stop! This moo's for you!" She was excited and giggling and hopping around like a pogo stick gone mad.

Edon stumbled through the door next. She was holding her stomach, doubled over with laughter. "Are you excited, Mason?" she asked, imitating the KDKD disc jockey. "No. I'm confused! *Confused!* I could've died, Mason. I never heard anything so-o-o funny."

I forgot about the trouble with Mrs. Essig and started grinning at Edon. Cristy walked into the room pointing a hairbrush at me. "You were priceless to-

day, Mason. Truly priceless. Did you practice those
lines? Trixie said you planned to say those things, but
I told her they were natural. They were natural,
weren't they, Mason? I mean, you really didn't know
what station you were calling, did you?'' Cristy looked
at Edon, who was now kicking her feet on the floor
and gasping for breath, and began to laugh herself. "It
was funny, wasn't it, Ed?"

Edon managed to nod her head.

"We aren't laughing at you, Mason," Cristy assured me between breaths.

"No, no," Edon cried. "We're laughing *with* you."

Dr. Essig came in and tried to settle everyone down.
Edon, Cristy and Melissa reenacted my conversation
word for word, and the doc couldn't help but join in
the hysteria. Someone would say something like "I'm
confused" or "What radio station is this?" and the
laughter would be renewed. We didn't settle down
until Mrs. Essig started bringing supper to the table.

That's when they found their presents. The excitement started all over again. No one cared that the
dinner was getting cold, not even Mrs. Essig, who
came to kiss me on the cheek for every gift that was
opened. Edon, Cristy and Melissa kissed me, too,
Edon and Cristy twice, and Melissa approximately
forty-seven times. My ears began to burn when they
started all the hugging. You'd have thought I'd bought
them all a house.

"This was very thoughtful of you, Mason," Dr.
Essig smiled and patted my arm affectionately.

"Yes, Mason. And it cost so much money!" Mrs.
Essig added.

"I'm sure he shopped at dirt cheap sales," Edon cut in.

"Ed! Don't be so ungrateful and rude!" Mrs. Essig didn't know her daughter was only trying to help me.

"It's okay. Edon's right. I did buy the TV on sale. I just wanted to show my appreciation for all the things you've done for me. Are you sure you like the skates, Melissa?"

She kissed me another forty-seven times. "Are you kidding? Can I try them out, please, Mom? Puleese?"

"After dinner, honey. Are you sure you didn't spend too much money, Mason? You must've used every cent you had."

Dr. Essig turned to look at me.

Edon forced a laugh. "Who's being rude now, Mom?"

"Ed's right, Mom. You shouldn't look a gift horse in the mouth. I know I certainly don't." Cristy flashed her perfect smile at me.

"Are you callin' Mason a horse?" Melissa demanded.

Everyone laughed, and the price tags weren't mentioned again. I really had a good time that night. It reminded me of my first weeks at the cabin before all the troubles had started. I even felt as though the doc and I were friends again.

But the next morning, when I started calling the local television stations and no one knew anything about a missing balloon, my frustration came back. I'd tried everything but the newspapers at the library.

I was running out of leads again.

I thought about talking to Dr. Essig—confronting him and using him as a lead. I'd say something like, *Dr. Essig, you don't have to worry about me telling anyone about this. I understand your position, and I have only a few hard feelings. What kind of information have you been withholding from me?*

Or maybe I'd use something stronger. *Okay, Doc, I know you're not telling me everything you know about my parents. Talk or I walk. I've got a friend. Officer Penners. He'll make sure the information gets out!*

I went to the library instead. The doc had been too kind to me. I could never turn him in, even if he was going vacant upstairs. I couldn't confront him either. If I was wrong, I'd feel like the ground of a Texas stockyard. It would be too horrible even to imagine.

Edon offered to help me at the library, and I accepted. We went through paper after paper until our hands were black. We didn't find anything about me, but we did discover a story about a balloon in New Mexico. It had been flying on too hot a day and was trying to make it above a mountain range besides. The envelope had caught fire, and the pilot, along with two passengers, had plummeted thousands of feet to the earth. The gondola was found rammed seven inches into the ground. It had penetrated the earth like the head of a sledgehammer.

Edon said she didn't know balloons had accidents. I told her hot air balloons were much safer than the old gas ones of the turn of the century or, perhaps, pilots were more educated about their crafts. But things were safer nowadays. The gruesome crash in New Mexico didn't deter Edon's enthusiasm to fly though. She was still looking forward to the next time

I went up, and we were talking about it more and more.

We broke for lunch at one o'clock. We washed up in the rest rooms, and I called for a taxi. I told Edon I was taking her to Bert's Corral, one of the nicer steak houses in Phoenix. We ordered appetizers before our meal and had cheesecake topped with strawberries for dessert.

"I think I like hanging around rich guys." Edon dunked a fried mushroom in some buttermilk dip and popped it into her mouth.

"I didn't know you could eat so much. Maybe I should be more selective of my luncheon dates."

Edon swallowed and looked hurt. "But I only ate as much as you did."

"I know." I put thirty-five dollars on the receipt plate. "I don't get much of a chance to tease you about your eating habits. My appetite usually out-shines yours so much."

"Outshines? How about *blinds*." She glanced at the tip and then fluffed at her hair. "How about we go kill a little time at the malls, big boy?"

"Love to, my little spendthrift, but I promised Melissa I'd go to Puppies and Things and pick out our new pet today." The waiter was happy to call a cab for us, and we headed across town. I was glad that Edon was with me. If I'd been alone at the library, I'd be feeling pretty low about now. But she wasn't giving me much time to think about things. She kept the conversation going and was joking around a lot. She told the taxi driver that I was wealthy, and that if he speeded it up some, I'd give him a twenty-dollar tip. I jerked her over beside me and was really going to let her have it, but the taxi driver hit the accelerator so fast that I didn't get the chance to say a word. He started running yellow lights and taking corners at about two hundred miles an hour. Edon and I banged against one door and then the other, and neither of us was able to remain still long enough to finish a sentence.

Finally he screeched to a halt. I threw some money over the front seat, and Edon and I stumbled onto the sidewalk.

"Are you nuts?" I demanded, turning my neck and massaging it with my fingers.

"I just wanted to see if he'd do it. Everyone's always paying taxis to speed it up in the movies. How was I to know that they go even faster in real life?"

"Well, don't do it again! Things are always worse in real life." I grabbed her hand and pulled her into the pet shop.

It smelled rank. Kind of like a zoo without any breeze going through. A round red-cheeked woman with silver hair and green plastic jewelry greeted us from behind a counter and told us to look around as much as we liked. A parrot walked back and forth on a wooden perch beside her. "Hello, hello, good-looking! Hey, you! Hello!" it squawked.

"Hello," Edon giggled back.

"How do you know he wasn't talking to me?" I whispered. She pushed me to the cages toward the rear of the store. Mrs. Essig said I could choose anything I liked outside of the reptile and rodent families. Edon wouldn't let me consider any fish because the Essigs had always had fish and this was the first time "in the history of the Essig children" that they were allowed to have anything that "breathed air, was larger than three inches and didn't lay eggs to reproduce."

I slowed down as we passed several aquariums with turtles in them. "They're kind of interesting."

"Keep walking."

"Hey, who's supposed to be doing the choosing anyway?"

"We've been waiting too long for this, Mason. I'm not going to let you blow it on an amphibian."

"Look! Baby tarantulas!"

"Disgusting. Over there, Mason. The bigger cages."

We walked to where the pet store began smelling stronger, directly past the snakes and guinea pigs, to the kittens and puppies. They were enclosed behind glass, different breeds separated into different enclosures.

The puppies that were awake bounced to the window and wagged their tails furiously.

"This is going to make me feel like a bum," I whispered, as if puppies could hear. We were only going to pick one, if any, and the rest, no matter how badly they wanted to come, would have to stay behind.

"I know what you mean. I can't count how many times I would go to a pet store as a kid just dying to see these little guys and then leave the place feeling like a crummy puppy dog deserter." She smiled brightly. "But this time we're going to be taking one with us. Unless, of course, you still want to get a stupid turtle."

I looked at the brown eyes staring back at me. The turtles wouldn't care if I walked away. The tarantulas had probably never even seen me. But these fellows here, they wanted out. "Okay. So which one? And who's going to tell the others they didn't pass the audition?''

"I will. But you pick the one you want. After all, this moo's for you." Edon studied the cages. "How about this Yorkshire terrier? He looks as though he could fit in a tea cup."

"Too small. Someone could step on him."

"This wienie dog is cute."

"Nope. Someone might cook him."

"Come on, Mason. Be serious. Pick one you like."

I sighed at the unfair task before me. All of them were pawing against the glass, as well as wiggling around and whining for attention. They were trying so hard that I couldn't help but notice the one who wasn't—an overgrown Saint Bernard, the only pup who was awake and not going crazy at the window.

I tapped the glass. "What do you think is wrong with him?"

Edon leaned closer. "I don't know. He looks depressed."

"Do you suppose he's sick?"

"Maybe. Why don't I ask the lady behind the counter?"

Edon left, and I tried to coax the puppy to the window. I made a lot of kissing sounds, clicked my fingers and cooed "come on, boy, come on, boy," generally making a fool of myself, and he just gazed at me, looking bored.

"He's not sick," Edon announced. "The lady said he's getting a bad attitude because he's been here so long. Most of the people in this area own townhouses or live in apartments, and they don't have enough room for a Saint Bernard. She says she'll cut the price fifty dollars if we take him, but I didn't tell her about the KDKD certificate."

He laid his sad-looking face on his giant paws.

"What do you think, Mason?"

"I don't know. I feel sorry for him. But I say he should show some effort on his part. Look at the others. They're going crazy."

"Okay. Try calling him to the glass one more time. If he gets up, we'll take him, if he doesn't, then it's his own lazy fault."

Edon and I tried to lure him to the window. She held up a Kleenex from her purse and started wiggling it around. I grabbed a big rubber bone from a nearby stand and started banging it on the enclosure. "Come on, boy! Come on, boy! Get up, stupid puppy! Come on, boy!"

He lifted his head, watching us with increasing interest, but still didn't move.

I pressed my finger against the glass. "Okay, dog, this is your last chance. We don't want no mutt with no bad attitude. Either you get off your butt or you can stay in this box until your hair falls out."

We stared at each other a few seconds, and he lifted his ears lazily. Then, to my amazement, he pulled himself to a standing position. He walked slowly to the window, plopped down again and pressed his nose against the window where my finger was. It was big and wet and looked gross smashed against the glass. He was grinning at us.

"How cute! How funny! How adorable! He wants to come, Mason! He's a comedian! We have a dog! I can't believe it. We really have a dog!" Edon chirped excitedly.

The puppy wouldn't stay in his box on the way home, and I had to pay the cabdriver thirty extra dollars to have his carpet cleaned because the pup didn't want to wait to relieve himself.

He really did have a bad attitude. And that's what we decided to name him—B.A. We let B.A. run around on the front lawn for a while, hoping he'd burn off some of his newfound energy before we took him inside to meet the rest of the family.

Edon thought he was the most magnificent beast ever to walk the earth. She glanced at me as we were about to walk inside, and I'm not sure why, but I leaned down and kissed her.

Her complexion flushed pink and, for once, she didn't have anything to say.

"Thanks for a very nice day, Edon," I whispered. "Thank you for everything."

Chapter Seven

A dog! A dog! A dog!" Melissa ran through the house like an Indian announcing the cavalry.

"How cuuuuute!" Cristy hurried over and scooped the squirming ball of fur into her arms. "So she's ours, Mason! Are we going to keep her?"

"If your mom says it's okay."

"She already has," Edon corrected. She began helping Cristy to press B.A.'s hair flat.

"What are we going to call him?"

"Call what?" Mrs. Essig squeezed between me and the girls. She stared at B.A. "Good grief," she half whispered. "It's one of those snow dogs that carries whiskey kegs around its neck."

"That's right, Mom. The courageous breed is called Saint Bernard. They've saved countless lives in the

Swiss Alps by searching out lost travelers." Edon lifted
B.A.'s head to make him appear more noble.

"How do you know that?"

"The pet store saleswoman."

"Well, did the pet store saleswoman also tell you
that Saint Bernards grow to the size of horses?"

"Not horses, Mom." Edon laughed. "Only ponies."

"Oh, excuse me, ponies." She sighed. "When I said
Mason could get a dog, I was thinking along the lines
of something weighing and eating less than a hundred
pounds a day."

"I'll be happy to pay for his food, Martha," I interrupted quickly.

"No, no, I didn't mean that."

"Look at his eyes, Mom. Here, let's watch him
walk." Cristy let him down.

He promptly squatted and left a puddle at her feet.

I grabbed him by the scruff of his neck, shoved his
nose in it, spanked him on the rump and took him
outside. "Boy, you sure know how to leave an
impression on people, don't you?" I scolded. He
started romping around, wanting to play, and accidentally fell into the pool.

It wasn't until after dinner that Mrs. Essig started
warming up to B.A. We were making sure he got outside in time, so there were no more accidents. Dr. Essig really liked him, which helped matters. After we'd
cleared the table, we all sat around the living room
watching Melissa play with him. She had a sock, and
he was yanking on it in a game of tug-of-war.

"Wayne sure would've liked B.A.," Cristy said out
of the blue.

The laughter stopped, and an awkward silence followed. Regret came into Cristy's eyes. Tears came into Martha's.

I wanted to shout, "It's okay! Go ahead and talk about him! You don't have to forget dead people. You can't! *Talk about Wayne!*

"You're right, Cristy. Wayne always liked dogs." Edon glanced at her father, then looked down at the carpet.

Mrs. Essig wiped her eyes. Dr. Essig rubbed his mustache. "He liked them until Mrs. Henshaw's poodle bit him in the ankle."

"He sure was nervous about walking past her house after that." Edon seemed uncertain. "Remember, Dad?"

He nodded. "Every year Wayne wanted me to call Mrs. Henshaw and make sure she was keeping current on its rabies shots."

"Did he really?" Cristy's eyes were filled with affection.

"One year I actually did it. Wayne had me convinced that the mutt could jump the back fence if it got mad enough." Dr. Essig reached over and squeezed Mrs. Essig's hand. "Do you remember, Martha? Mrs. Henshaw was quite upset with me. I'm sure that's why she didn't invite us to the block party the following year."

"She's an old busybody anyway." Mrs. Essig gazed back at her husband. "She's just fortunate that Wayne was a good boy. He could've kicked the stupid dog right back over the fence if he hadn't been so considerate of animals."

They continued talking about Wayne a while longer, and I held my breath, waiting for something to go wrong, something to snap.

But it didn't. The Essigs were missing their son and talking about him, and no one was blaming anyone else.

The next morning at breakfast, Dr. Essig asked me about school. It was starting soon. The girls were already making plans for registration. He asked if I had any idea what year I was in, or if I thought I'd already graduated.

Naturally I wasn't much help. Dr. Essig had some tests done after we'd returned from camping, and we were able to determine my age to be around seventeen or eighteen, or maybe even nineteen. He didn't have any idea what my academic level was, however, and he suggested some additional testing to determine that as well. He said he wouldn't know where to enroll me otherwise, and that amnesia was no excuse for welshing on my education. If I'd forgotten a few million things, homework would help to remind me of them.

I just sat there, agreeing with everything he said. As long as I had time to continue the search for my parents, I didn't care what tests I took or what school I sat in.

After I fed B.A. and took him outside, I went to my room and hung around in there for a while. Edon had gone horseback riding with Julie, and Cristy had gone shopping with Trixie. Mrs. Essig had taken Melissa to the grocery store, and the doc had finally left for his office. It was just me and B.A.

And my problems.

Problems show up best when you're alone. I'd begun to notice that. It wasn't easy facing the fact that I was out of leads. I had no idea what to do next.

It was hard to understand why I hadn't become a news item. As far as anyone else knew, I was dead or was roaming around the mountains like Tarzan of the Grand Canyon raised by mules instead of monkeys. For some reason, my family was avoiding the media.

It didn't make sense. It was only logical that if you lose something, you advertise to find it. Unless there was some private detective combing the hills, the airwaves and papers seemed the best methods of locating someone.

It was depressing.

No. It was more than depressing. It was confusing and hopeless.

I kept going over what I knew and analyzing the facts, meditating on my situation and repeating it all again and again in my mind until finally I was in the gloomiest mood humanly possible. When Edon returned from riding, she wanted to come in my room to talk awhile, and I politely said no. Cristy knocked on the door and asked if I wanted to walk B.A. with her. I tactfully told her I preferred to stay where I was. Melissa invited me to watch *Mister Rogers*, and I explained that I'd rather undergo chemotherapy. I hibernated there all day. Even when Mrs. Essig called me for dinner, I didn't feel like coming out. My appetite, along with all hope, was gone.

The house became quiet after that. Until around eight o'clock. Then Edon called my name outside the door.

"I think I'm going to bed," I answered. "Can it wait until tomorrow?"

"No. It's an emergency."

I swung my legs over the bed and ran my fingers through my hair. I don't think I'd combed it all day.

"Surprise!" Edon and Cristy shouted when I opened the door.

There was a huge tree in front of me. It wasn't huge in terms of the wide open spaces, but it was pretty big for a house.

"Okay, Ed, bring it on in," Cristy instructed, waving her forward. I couldn't see Edon through the maze of leaves, but I knew she was there by the moans and groans that followed the plant in. "Do you like it?" Cristy asked.

"I'm not sure," I replied. "What's it for?"

"To look at, silly. Edon and I knew you were feeling down, so we thought we'd buy this tree to remind you of the mountains. You seemed to be happier when we were at the cabin." She glanced around the room, stopping Edon from coming around the tree. "Why don't you stay there till we figure out where to put it, Ed."

"It was a nice thought." I grinned at Cristy. I'd never seen her and Edon do anything together by choice. "But I don't know if I'll be able to keep it alive. I'm not even sure how to treat a plant."

"You can treat it anyway you want. Just don't water it." Edon tried to peek at me through the branches. "It's silk."

"What did you say, Edon? It's milk?" I tried to push some of the leaves out of the way. "Where are you anyway?"

"Here. Right here."

I ducked down and spotted a nose. Suddenly I remembered something that seemed from years ago.

My heart started drumming in my chest. It was an old thought. A memory from before! I straightened. My throat grew dry. Flashes of a past began zinging through my mind. *Don't panic!* I screamed inside my head. *Don't lose it!*

The acid feeling seeped into my stomach. I bent down to see Edon through the branches again.

"You're here," I half whispered. Another flash.

Edon hopped from behind the tree. "What's wrong? What's happening to him, Cristy?"

"I've seen you before. Both of you." I pointed at Edon. "You told me my balloon was flat." I turned to Cristy. "And you're the dream girl beamed down to Earth from Venus."

"Well, thank you, Mason. Someone else told me that once."

Edon stepped closer, staring at me. "Wait a minute! He's remembering us from when he crashed!" She shook my arm to help me out of my daze. "Aren't you, Mason? You're remembering us, aren't you?"

I nodded. I didn't want to speak, move, breathe too heavily, or do anything that might push the memories away. My heart was racing so fast that I felt dizzy.

"Go get Dad, quick!" Edon continued to watch my face closely.

"Oh, no! I think he's at the hospital. Do you think we should page him?"

"Yes! Yes! Tell him to call as soon as he can!"

Cristy flew from the room, her blond hair whipping back and forth behind her.

"Now concentrate, Mason. Concentrate." Edon led me gently to the bed. "Can you remember anything else?"

"The balloon landing. Crashing through the trees. I shouldn't have gone so far."

"Good. Concentrate. Keep concentrating." She was trying to make her tone calm, but I could tell she was as excited as I was.

My stomach felt sicker. "I didn't want to die. I really didn't want to die." Another flash.

"Of course not, Mason. No one wants to die."

"But I could've died. I didn't want to die."

Edon squeezed my hand. "Think of something else. You're scaring me."

"I didn't want to die, so I had to find a clearing. My reserve fuel was gone. I had to get somewhere fast."

"Why did you use all your fuel?"

Think! my voice was screaming inside my head. *More happened! Think of more!* "I don't know. It was gone. And the wind was so strong!"

"Your name, Mason. Can you remember your name?"

My name. Concentrate. My head was pounding. *What's my name? My name! What's my name?*

I fell backward on the bed, squeezing my head between my hands. "I can't remember. I'm trying, Edon, but I just can't remember."

A little while later, Dr. Essig studied me from across his desk. His office was just as I'd expected. Dustless, full of books, pictures of his family on every shelf. There were even a few plastic statues, probably presents from his kids. One said, World's Best Dad, and another read, Love Makes the World Go Round.

"One more time, Mason. Tell me everything you remember."

I moaned and leaned on my hand so that my elbows stretched across at least half the desk. We'd been over this three times. I remembered coming up a ridge of the Canyon, looking for a place to land, then crashing. I remembered trying to see Cristy better and the gondola becoming unbalanced. I remembered falling toward the ground, face first, and hearing the gondola smashing into the dirt.

I told him again.

"You don't remember anything else?" He leaned forward, his eyes becoming smaller. Intense. "Nothing at all?"

The doc had been the only member of the Essig family who hadn't acted absolutely out of their mind with excitement for me. Mrs. Essig had used an entire roll of film for the occasion. We were all nearly blinded. The doc appeared happy at first, but he began acting strangely after I'd explained what I could remember.

I'd never suspected him as much as I did now. He should've been pleased about the recall. Instead, he acted worried. I figured he was getting scared that I was going to remember it all soon.

I'd leave to go with my family then. People might discover he'd been lying. I didn't want anything bad to happen to the doc, but still, I wanted to find my parents.

"I told you before, Dr. Essig, I can't remember anything else."

"How did you feel when you had these memory flashes?"

"Sick to my stomach." *How do you feel when you lie to me?*

"I don't know, Mason." He started tapping a pencil against the desk, and his mustache twitched. "I don't like this."

I bet you don't.

"I'm afraid I'm going to call in a new specialist."

Sure you are.

"Do you have any objections?"

"None. Do whatever you like."

"I'm going to make an appointment for you. Tomorrow, nine o'clock sharp. Is that all right?"

He was really doing a number this time. I felt kind of sorry for him. Even though the Essigs were becoming a real family again, as he'd promised Mrs. Essig they would, he wouldn't let go. I wondered if he even knew what was real and what wasn't anymore. Sometimes I think he actually believed he was telling me the truth. "Sure, Doc. Nine's good for me."

"Dr. Bekins is his name. He's a doctor of psychiatry."

Psychiatry! I should've known. It was the perfect way of sending me to someone without sending me to anyone at all. A brain surgeon might be able to do something, but because my problem was physical and not emotional, a psychiatrist would be a real safe choice for someone who didn't want me cured.

I was onto his game now.

"He'll ask you some questions, Mason. Maybe have you take a few tests. Nothing to be nervous about."

"Oh, I'm not nervous. Not anymore, anyway." I straightened. "Listen, Doc, can I be excused now? I feel like I could sleep for a week."

Dr. Essig rubbed his neck. "Sure, son. It must be near midnight. Let me lock up, and we'll get out of here."

Mrs. Essig had taken the girls home about an hour ago. When Dr. Essig had found out about my memory return, he'd asked Mrs. Essig to drive me to his office immediately. He'd arrived from the hospital about fifteen minutes after we had, and I'd undergone two physical checkups and a bombardment of questions from about nine o'clock on.

Dr. Essig was quiet on the way home. I laid my head against the car seat and shut my eyes, hoping to sleep.

I was dancing inside! Now that I'd discovered I wasn't a lunkhead permanently, and that my amnesia really was temporary just as Dr. Essig had at first diagnosed, I felt as if nothing was impossible. It was only a matter of time now. I really believed that. Soon everything would come back like a great flood.

I let my imagination go.

I wondered if Cristy was right, and I'd find out that I was married. I laughed aloud, and Dr. Essig glanced at me. I didn't know enough about women. If I was married, I was definitely a newlywed.

I thought about school. Maybe I was already a college graduate. A genius-type whiz kid.

That was doubtful, too. But I did hope I was out of high school. Seeing Edon and Cristy in all their preparation for the new year wasn't exactly appealing. I wanted to be farther along in life. Maybe even have a good job—a vice president's position somewhere.

I laughed again, and the doc cleared his throat. He was probably thinking that the psychiatrist might be useful after all.

Life sure takes strange turns sometimes. Earlier that night I wouldn't have given a quarter for my future. The chances of finding my parents had seemed darker than a mine shaft. But now, only four short hours later, I had a galaxy of optimism. All I needed to do was relax and let the hours slip by until the next wall in my brain crumbled.

Chapter Eight

Dr. Bekins was the classic shrink: sloppy haircut, wire-rimmed glasses, brown tweed shirt with a tie that was bought on the planet Mars. He was nice enough, although he acted very insecure. And he stared a lot. Not the normal kind of staring that people do when they see something surprising. This was an intent staring, as if he were trying to pierce my head, open my mind and proofread my thoughts.

Uneasily I stared back.

For an hour and a half he asked questions. I answered them as well as I could, considering I only had ten weeks of memory with me.

"Would you consent to being put under hypnosis?" he inquired, his look reaching across the space between us like a giant corkscrew.

"I don't think so, Dr. Bekins."

He tried again just before it was time to leave. "I believe hypnosis would be most beneficial in this case. Are you sure you won't reconsider?"

"Absolutely. Where did you get your tie, sir?"

Edon and Cristy were waiting for me in the car. We'd decided to celebrate my unexpected recall with a picnic. The doc had to work, but everyone else was free. Edon said she would peek at me through the bushes until something else came back.

"Where's Martha?" I asked, sliding into the front seat beside Edon.

"Dad said this would take a while, so she went ahead to get a picnic table." Cristy glanced in the rearview mirror and pulled from the curb into the flow of traffic.

Edon was fidgeting around. She'd find a song on the radio, listen to two or three words, then push a button to another song. Her feet kept bumping into mine. She was trying hard not to look at me.

I let her squirm for a few more minutes.

"Since when did you become so tactful?" I finally asked.

"What do you mean?" She immediately flicked off the radio. Ready.

"If you want to know how it went at Dr. Bekins's office, why don't you just ask me? You always said what you wanted to in the past."

"He's right, Ed. You might as well ask him. I'm certainly not going to. I've always had manners," Cristy said.

Edon squared her shoulders. "Okay, fine. Far be it from me to try and change. If you want me to be rude. Okay. Fine. I'll be rude." She turned to me, her green eyes wide and flashing. "So tell me, Mason Redford from Moscow, what did the shrink have to say about you?"

I tweaked her cheek. "That's the girl we all know and love."

Cristy momentarily closed her eyes and shook her head.

"He didn't say anything."

Both girls looked disappointed.

"Beady-eyed Bekins wants to talk to your dad before he gives an opinion. But I'm pretty sure he's going to recommend padded walls."

Edon punched me in the arm.

"Well, what were you expecting him to say?"

"I don't know." She exchanged glances with Cristy. "We're not sure why Dad wanted you to see Dr. Bekins in the first place."

He did it to make you think he was trying to help me. Good job, huh?

"We don't understand how a psychiatrist can do anything for you."

That makes three of us.

I could've exposed the doc right then and there but, as I said before, I didn't mean him any harm. The doc needed a shrink of his own, not more trouble from his family. He'd been kind to me, and I was going to hate to see what happened when he was found out and his lies were uncovered. "Your dad is probably hoping that Dr. Bekins can help me cope with my memory return. If it all comes at once, I might flip out. I might be too wonderful for me to handle."

They giggled, and I started singing, "I ain't nuthin' but a hound dog," hoping to imitate Elvis Presley but actually sounding more like a real dog.

We drove down a road that had been cut between two mountains next to a desert stream that ran underground seven months out of the year. It was a beautiful canyon full of birds, lizards and squirrels. I recognized it instantly, and I knew I'd been there many times before.

We found Mrs. Essig in a secluded area where the stream formed a small pond. Tall mesquites and cottonwoods shaded a cement table and a wide clearing around it. Melissa scrambled up the rocky slope to meet us on the road.

"We unloaded the car. We did everything. We walked and walked and walked. I think my legs are broken!"

I lifted her and carried her on my shoulders to the table. Mrs. Essig had prepared a big lunch, and I was starved. I'd skipped dinner last night and I'd overslept this morning, missing breakfast.

I ate one of the two chickens she'd fried and at least half of the cake. Edon said I'd outdone myself this time. Afterward we took a hike, and she kept hurrying ahead of me, hiding herself in thickets until I'd walk by. She'd begin a conversation with me so that I'd have to find her through the branches.

"Ouch! This stick keeps poking me. So, Mason," she called. "Do you think it's going to rain? Ouch!"

"Why don't you give up, honey?" Martha sat on a nearby tree trunk to rest. "You're getting yourself all scratched up. You'll probably get a cactus in you."

"But it worked once. It's what helped him to re-member everything. Wasn't it, Mason?"

"She's got a point, Martha." I ducked down to peer through a maze of sticks. "What's that I see?" I bent lower. "A coyote? A rat?"

"A rat?" Melissa hurried over.

"Come on, Mason. Do it right. You're supposed to say 'Where are you?' and I'm supposed to say 'Here. Right here.' Now come on. Ouch! Say it."

"Where are you?"

"Here. Ouch. Right here."

I straightened, the smile disappearing from my face.

"He's remembering something!" Cristy cried.

Mrs. Essig rushed over. Melissa started bouncing up and down. "What is it?" Edon shouted from behind the bush. "What's going on?"

"I think I was bitten by something." I lifted my Levi's and looked at my ankle.

Everyone moaned and walked away.

"Hey! This could be serious. There's a red spot be-low my ankle!"

Melissa returned and squatted down to study my foot. "There's a baby ant down here. A red one," she announced.

"I've got it!" Edon crawled from the bushes and dusted herself off. "We need to go back farther. Be-fore the balloon crash. We need to go up in the bal-loon!"

"She's right!" Cristy joined in excitedly. "It's a perfect idea!"

"It sounds logical," Mrs. Essig agreed cautiously. "But it seems so dangerous. If something happened up there and Mason got hurt again…" She glanced at me, frown lines filling her forehead.

"I'd fly on a clear, calm day, away from the city, near the fields where it's easy to land." I was even more excited than the girls. I ruffled Melissa's hair. "There's nothing to worry about, Martha. It's absolutely safe if you know what you're doing."

Edon cleared her throat and looked away.

"I'll check the envelope and burner system thoroughly. The gondola landed on its bottom. There's no trace of damage to it."

"I don't know, Mason. It sounds so risky." She took Melissa's hand and started up the path. "We'll talk to Eric about it. We'll see what he says."

"Absolutely not!" Dr. Essig tromped around the living room like a bull daring someone to challenge him.

Edon spoke first. Very softly. "Our reasoning is extremely sound, Dad. It was a familiar situation, an exact reenactment almost that sparked Mason's memory yesterday. It's only logical that a balloon flight would do the same thing again."

"Yes, dear, I understand that." The doc's face was hard. "But Mason's memory will return when it's ready. It doesn't need to be pushed by dangerous escapades in the sky."

"I don't think hot air balloons qualify as 'dangerous escapades,'" I said quietly.

He looked at me in surprise. I realized then that I'd never spoken back to the doc.

"Quite true, Mason. A craft passing all the safety standards of the FAA could be considered all right, but your balloon has crashed once."

"They're made specifically to withstand hard landings."

"Would you excuse us please? I think Mason and I should discuss this privately." Dr. Essig ignored everyone's amazed expressions and waited silently for his family to file out of the room. Once he and I were alone, he sat down in the soft winged chair in front of me.

"I get the distinct feeling you and I are disagreeing on this flying excursion," he said.

"Yes, sir."

"Although, I can't explain all of them to you, I think you should know I have some very sound reasons for my decision."

Sure. Like it might really work.

He leaned forward, folding his hands across his lap. "I spoke with Dr. Bekins today, and I think, as your doctor and guardian, that I should explain what he told me." He paused, staring at me the same way Dr. Bekins had. He was acting quite solemn, so I played my part and attempted to look concerned—or at least curious.

"Dr. Bekins is of the opinion that your amnesia is the effect of something emotional, not physical."

"I don't understand."

"You see, we always assumed that your memory blockage was a direct result of your fall. That it was caused by a physical blow to the head area." He shrugged. "It was an obvious guess. But Dr. Bekins feels your memory loss is forced. That for unknown reasons, you're causing the blockage yourself, not wanting to deal with an event in the past. Believe it or not, it's a common type of amnesia. Of course, he can't be positive after only one session, and he's not going to make a formal diagnosis yet, but he's quite sure of himself. He gave me enough reasons to consider it and enough proof to believe it."

I kept any crazy expressions from showing on my face so that the doc wouldn't get suspicious. Besides being stupid, I pondered on how convenient this little theory was for him. Why try any further physical treatments when I'm diagnosed emotional? No, Dr. Essig was out, and Dr. Bekins, along with hypnosis and head games, was in.

I'd never be cured.

"Excuse me, Doc," I said, managing to keep the sarcasm from my voice. "Exactly what reasons did Dr. Bekins give you for this conclusion."

"There were several. He's asked me to keep some of them confidential until he had additional time with you. But a few of the more typical ones are your categories of recall: places, people outside your immediate realm of security, learned abilities, and other *impersonal* parts of life. Also, the pattern of your recall. You don't remember small sections of all your life, but rather, the entire section of a small part of your life." He sighed. "And then there's the time element. Loss of memory from physical blows to the head usually returns sooner than this."

"Sounds very believable, Doc."

He looked at me curiously.

Maybe it was the wrong thing to say. Or perhaps I hadn't been able to keep the sarcasm from my tone after all.

"Of course it's believable. Dr. Bekins is highly respected in his field. I think he can really help you."

"Whatever you say, Dr. Essig."

"I don't want you to let this discourage you, Mason."

"Oh, it's not. Emotional, physical, who cares as long as I get my memory back soon." I watched the doc's face for a response. I thought the word "soon" might give him a jolt. He seemed pleased though, as if he really appreciated my attitude. And why not? I was like an obedient dog being led to the pound. Whatever he said, I did. Whatever he diagnosed, I never doubted. I didn't argue, object or complain.

"Will that be all, Doc?"

We stood, and he put his arm around me. "Did I ever tell you how much I appreciate you, Mason?

I immediately looked down.

"I'm not one for the mushy stuff, but I want you to know that we really care for you, son. We didn't have much hope until you came into our lives. You've helped us more than we've helped you, even with all your bumps and bruises." He brushed at his eye. "You're a good boy, Mason."

Later, I lay in bed, staring at the stucco ceiling. The moonlight had changed it to a shade of gray. I was thinking over everything that had happened, including my conversation with Dr. Essig. I knew that he was guilty, and yet I couldn't bring myself to hate him. I couldn't even dislike him. He'd meant what he'd said. He really cared about me.

I wasn't making excuses for him. What he was doing was wrong. He could go to jail for it, or lose his license as a doctor. I'd known that when I was talking to Officer Penners, which is why I'd never called him back. I didn't want to see the doc suffer for his deceptions. I figured it wasn't really his fault. The sadness over the loss of his son was too much to handle. Somehow I understood that.

In fact, I wanted to *keep* the doc out of trouble. He wasn't well. He'd blown a fuse. It wouldn't be hard if I was clever about it. I wouldn't tell anyone about my next recall. I'd find my parents alone and explain everything to them. Because the media didn't know about me, no one else was involved.

Except maybe Officer Penners with the missing person reports. I was sure my parents wouldn't press charges if they knew the whole story. If the police understood all the circumstances, they'd drop the whole thing, too.

Easy on the doc. That's what I was concerned with now. How to make it easy on the doc. Going back to my family would be difficult for him to accept. My parents, I was sure, would be willing to help. I knew they wouldn't care how often I visited. After all, the Essigs had saved my life.

It had been a hard day, emotionally speaking, and I was getting tired. I formed the plan one last time in my mind. I would make sure I kept my next recall secret. I would locate my parents myself and explain the whole story to them. They would assist me in keeping the doc out of trouble. We would help him get better.

I yawned and gently dropped B.A.'s sleeping body to the floor. He hardly stirred. I hadn't mentioned the balloon flight to Dr. Essig since our initial discussion. I'd protested his decision in front of the others and only once when we were alone. Disagreeing with him didn't matter anymore as far as I could see.

I was going up, and no one was going to stop me.

Chapter Nine

Edon was sitting on the edge of the pool, dangling her feet in the water, watching me out of the corner of her eye. I did a cannonball dive, and a stream of water shot above her. Her hair was dripping when I came up for air, but she acted as if it didn't bother her.

"Come on, spitfire! Get even with me!" I sent another bucket of water at her.

She shut her eyes and turned her head, but she didn't try to defend herself.

"Ah, come on." I hopped out of the pool beside her. "It's no fun provoking someone if they don't attack back."

"I'm thinking."

"About the balloon flight?"

She nodded. "I don't know about disobeying Dad like that. I mean, it's one thing to sneak in a televi-

sion show when you should be doing homework, but
leaving the earth . . . It seems as if you should get permission to do something like that.''

B.A. galloped across the patio and plopped down
beside us. I wiggled my fingers, and he started gnaw-
ing on them. Edon was making me uneasy. Maybe I
shouldn't have told her that I was going up. She
sounded as though she might inform the doc.

"You've never snuck behind his back before," she
said.

"What do you call the hundred thousand dollars?''

"That's not sneaking! You aren't disobeying anyone by keeping it. You're simply not telling all you
know. When you fly your balloon, you're not only
sneaking, you're deliberately going against Dad's will.
And risking your life, too!''

"Oh, wonderful. Now you're sounding like your
father.''

She glared at me. "What's wrong with that?''

I ruffled B.A.'s ears, trying to make our discussion
appear more casual than it really was. I couldn't tell
her that I had excellent reasons for sneaking a flight,
that her father wasn't thinking straight anymore, that
he was unstable and untrustworthy, and that I couldn't
accept his judgment any more than a perfect stranger's. "It's not dangerous, that's all. We'll inflate the
envelope and check it thoroughly for damage before I
go up.''

"Don't you feel the least bit bad about this?''

"No. Ow!" B.A. had chomped down too hard,
forgetting I was his master and not a bone. "If I'd
known you were going to be so worried about it, I

wouldn't have told you." I pushed the rambunctious
pup away.

"But I thought you needed my help."

"I do need your help. And Cristy's and Trixie's, and
Julie's, too. I'm going to need all of you for a ground
crew." We were quiet for a few seconds. "It was your
idea to go up in the first place, remember? You were
so sure it would work."

"And I still think it would, but—" She bit her bottom lip, knowing she'd just given me the edge I
needed.

"Then shouldn't I try? Wouldn't you if you were in
my place?"

"But what if something happens? What if you crash
again?"

"Maybe my memory will be knocked back. Looks
as if I can't lose either way." I grinned at her, but she
still wasn't ready to give in. "Nothing's going to happen, Edon. I promise you. It's almost as safe as riding a bike."

"Wayne broke his leg once while riding a bike."

"So that's it. Wayne again. You're worried that
what happened to your brother is going to happen to
me. That I'm going to kill myse—" I stopped when I
saw Edon's horrified expression. She scrambled to her
feet and started away. "Wait! Edon! I'm sorry!" How
could I have said something so stupid! There were
hundreds of other ways I could've expressed myself,
or better yet, not at all. "Please, Edon! I really didn't
mean to be such a moron!"

She slowed down and then stopped. Finally she
turned to face me. "But you're right, Mason. That's
exactly what I do think. I don't want to lose you.

Wayne didn't mean to die either, and if Dad says it's not safe to go up, then I say it's not safe to go up." She swung around and continued toward the patio. "But I'm going to help you, Mason Redford from Moscow, 'cause you think it's so-o-o important to remember everything right this minute." She opened the sliding glass door, stepped inside and turned to face me again. "But I want you to know it's against my better judgment. In fact, it's against all my judgment." She slid the door shut and walked away.

Cristy was more agreeable to my plan, but not by great lengths. She was also worried that Dr. Essig might be right, that he had some keen reason, some inside secret knowledge on the dangers of ballooning that none of the rest of us knew about. Their anxiety was understandable, considering what had happened to Wayne. But they weren't listening to reason. They were too afraid another tragedy might happen.

It was funny. I wished they could see themselves. They were acting exactly like their parents. All Cristy's complaining about her mother and father "smothering" her with so much protection that she "couldn't breathe" and look at her! She was doing a perfect imitation of them!

It was hard to believe that she was the same girl who'd diagnosed her parents as paranoid, the same rebellious daughter whose shocking suspicions of her father had proved to be true. I'm not sure why I didn't tell her about the doc. It could've been the same old reason I never told any of them anything that might cause tension. I still liked the Essigs best as the peaceful, Mr. and Mrs. Harmony and family. Cristy was getting along with her parents really well these days. I didn't want to stir up old feelings.

When I told them I wouldn't be flying right away, they relaxed a little. I needed time to dig up some ground equipment. All I had was the envelope, gondola and burners. I needed an inflation fan and a trailer to haul the stuff around. Without them I wasn't going anywhere.

I wondered where my original equipment was and my last launching site. It was impossible to guess the exact spot, but from what I could remember of the flight, I'd come from the east somewhere.

I called a local balloon club and asked if they knew where I might be able to purchase a fan and a trailer. A lady called Vi told me of a man who was selling his entire rig. She didn't know if he'd be willing to piece it out, but she gave me his name and number and said I should give it a try. While I had her on the line, I asked her, as matter-of-factly as I could, if she'd heard anything about any missing balloons lately. She said, "No, dear," and didn't make me feel too stupid about it. After I hung up, I immediately called Mr. Cady, the man she'd told me about. I made an appointment to look at his rig that afternoon while the doc was at work and Mrs. Essig was doing her shopping. I asked Edon if she wanted to come along. I couldn't ask Cristy to join us because of the money. If she knew how much cash was needed for the ground equipment, she'd think I'd been robbing liquor stores at night.

We headed out the door about five minutes after Mrs. Essig. I hurried to Cristy's car and got in the

driver's side. Edon stood in front of it, staring at me
through the windshield.

"What are you doing, Mason?" she inquired, a
smile beginning at the corners of her mouth.

I thought for a moment. What *was* I doing? I
opened the door and stepped out. "I guess I was going
to drive."

"You know how to drive, huh?"

"So it appears." I hadn't even thought about it. I'd
walked to Cristy's car, gotten in and grabbed for the
ignition as if I'd been doing it my whole life.

"I bet you have a license," Edon said, watching me
thoughtfully.

"Not on me." I knew she was thinking how convenient it would be if we drove ourselves instead of taking the bus, but I wasn't going to risk it. Who knew
what might happen if the police stopped us! They'd
ask my name, and I'd say Mason Redford. Then
they'd call it in on the radio and do an identity check,
and there would be no such person, no license under
that name. They'd say I was getting smart with them
and would demand my real name, and I'd reply I
didn't know my real name. They'd knock me around,
take me in, book me...

"We're getting a bus."

Edon's point was only momentary. "Better hurry
then or we'll miss it and have to wait for a cab." We
jogged all the way to the bus stop.

Mr. Cady didn't live too far away. He was waiting
for us and opened the front door before we even had
a chance to knock. He appeared disappointed. I think
it was our age.

I introduced Edon and myself, and he escorted us to his garage. He had a setup that looked brand-new. He switched on the fan, and we tried out the burners, which made Edon jump about a foot in the air. We turned everything off again when it was time to talk terms.

"I'm asking nine thousand, and that's a rock-bottom bargain price. If you've been shopping, you'd know that."

"Yes, sir, that's a reasonable price. Your rig's in good shape."

"Good shape?" He raised his hands above his head as if he were holding up a beach ball. "Why the dern thing's never been used more than ten times. I bought it because I figured it would be an interesting hobby. Huh. Last time I flew, a wind came up outta nowhere, and I nearly found myself a yo-yo in some electric lines."

"Could that hurt you?" Edon asked.

"Are you kidding, little lady? Hit them hot wires and the colonel could sell you for Sunday dinner. I don't need a hobby like that."

She looked at me, her lips drawing into a tight line. "Is he talking about fried chicken?"

"Fried chicken, fried steak, fried liver. That's what I'm talking about." He forced a laugh. "Now I don't want to be scarin' you folks off. Flying can be a lotta fun. All kinds of people are doing it, and nuthin's happened to them except, of course, for that one fella in Paris."

"What fella?" Edon squeaked.

"You know, the man who had to jump." He shook his head. "And right when he was about to make it over that skyscraper, too. Bodies don't smash apart like eggs, ya know. They stay together and just kinda 'thud' a couple of inches in the dirt.''

Edon collapsed on a pile of tires.

"We're not worried about that, Mr. Cady," I assured him. He glanced at Edon. "I've been flying for a while now. I already own a balloon. What I need to purchase is some ground equipment. A trailer and your gas fan."

"You want me to piece this stuff out?"

"Well, we're not interested in buying it all."

He rubbed his forehead as he thought about it. "I was kinda hoping to sell the whole thing together. That's how I bought it."

I nodded.

"I dunno much about piecing it out. I'm not sure I could find buyers for it all. Do folks do that very often?"

Edon shook her head no.

I told him I wasn't sure.

"I guess I shouldn't then. Not until I find out more about it."

Edon hopped off the tires. "Well, you tried, Mason. We better go now." She sounded like a kid who'd just found out she could keep her tonsils after all.

"Wait a second, folks. If I dropped the price to eight thousand, would you think about it some?" Mr. Cady asked.

"Yes, sir, I would." Eight thousand dollars didn't seem an unreasonable sum to pay for the memory I needed to find my family. It would keep Dr. Essig from getting himself any further into trouble, too.

Yes, the more I thought about it, the more it sounded like a bargain. "You have yourself a deal, Mr. Cady."

"Mason!" Edon gasped.

I rented a storage room the next morning and had Mr. Cady drop the rig off there. I separated the things I needed so we could pick them up without complications. After talking it over with Edon and Cristy, we decided the following Friday would be the best day to launch. We told Mrs. Essig that we were adventuring on an all-day excursion, and we wanted to get a very early start. Because of the summer temperatures, I needed to launch the balloon no later than six-thirty in the morning.

Mrs. Essig thought we were talking about a vigorous dawn hike up a desert canyon. She wasn't too excited about letting us go alone without herself, or Dr. Essig, but she'd been trying to loosen her restrictions on the girls. You could see that her heart wanted to say no, but her lips went ahead and said yes. It was a big step for her. A giant change from the way she'd been at the cabin.

If Mrs. Essig knew what we were really going to do, she'd need CPR.

Edon made sure the time was okay for Julie, and Cristy cleared it with Trixie. I also arranged for several practice sessions where we could stretch out the envelope and I could explain everyone's duties. It would give me a chance to test the burner system for leaks and to check the cables and struts.

The first practice session was on Tuesday. Trixie was late, and Julie said she had to leave early. I tried to keep the atmosphere positive, even though things weren't starting out well. I thought the best way of handling the training was for me to take an instructor's position. I opened with a lecture on the history of ballooning, beginning in the eighteen hundreds. But soon I could see the girls were forcing themselves to stay interested. They became more inspired when I talked about Madame Johnson, the first female ever to fly in a balloon. I'd checked out a book on ballooning from the library and read her story from that.

Cristy raised her hand as though she were in class.

I responded like a serious professor. It was my first question. "Yes, Ms. Essig?"

"What was Madame Johnson wearing?"

The girls giggled.

I checked the reference and was surprised to find that her dress really had been noted in the historical event. I guess fashion-minded people lived in the eighteen hundreds as well as in the eighties. "She wore white satin," I replied.

Everyone ooohed, so I figured they thought Madame Johnson's outfit was chic enough. "However, we'll wear heavy-duty gloves and cotton. It's safer."

They booed me, and I continued my history lesson until they started throwing pieces of grass and pebbles at me. "Do we have a problem?" I finally asked, ducking a weed.

"We want to learn how to inflate a balloon, not memorize who invented them," Trixie complained.

"A ground crew should have some academic knowledge on ballooning history as well as physical know-how," I explained patiently.

A rock smashed my toe.

"Okay. Let's move on to the envelope itself." I demonstrated how to remove the envelope from the canvas bag. "It's size is always impressive. You keep pulling and pulling and pulling material out. It reminds you of a magician yanking a long string of handkerchiefs from a top hat."

"How are we ever going to fill that thing with air?" Julie asked in amazement.

"There was a time when people did it entirely themselves by taking a hold of the throat of the balloon and flopping it up and down to get the air inside. You needed the arms of King Kong to succeed, but now—" I paused and lifted the gas-powered fan from the trailer "—we have this. Ta da!"

"Oh, boy! Air-conditioning!" Cristy moved closer.

"I see. Something to keep us cool while we flap!" Julie said.

Edon shook her head in disgust. "No, bozos. It's a fan to blow air *into* the envelope, not on us."

They applauded gratefully, and I trudged onward. Trixie kept stepping on the material until I finally threatened to take her up with me if she did it again. That particular warning worked really well with all of them. As exciting as ballooning looked, none of the girls were planning on flying with me. Edon said it might have something to do with the fact that I crashed during my last flight and they were waiting to see how it went this time.

I named all the parts of the envelope and gondola so that when I told someone to grab something she'd know what I was talking about. I also explained the procedure of a flight and what I expected everyone to do. We kept rehearsing certain parts until I felt it was ingrained enough to stop. It went okay, considering it was everyone's first attempt as a ground crew. However, if the burners had really been lit, I was sure we would've caught the whole thing on fire at least twice.

We packed up around noon, and I took everyone to lunch at a pizza place. Cristy kept bringing Madame Johnson into the conversation, saying it would be absolutely adorable if the girls could have matching outfits to wear. Satin overalls with white gloves.

The second session went much better. We got permission to inflate the balloon on the grassy lawn of a health club outside the city limits. I used the fan for a partial inflation to give everyone the feel of an authentic flight procedure. It looked huge even at half size. The girls were in awe. While two of them practiced holding the mouth of the envelope open to the stream of air, I showed the others how to tend to the envelope as it grew and became buoyant.

We drew quite a crowd. Cristy said we would've looked much more impressive if we'd had the matching outfits. The people were visibly disappointed when they discovered that we were only having a training session for the ground crew and we wouldn't be flying.

It made us nervous. I'd read a story from our balloon book about a Frenchman named Michel who was preparing for a balloon flight demonstration in Philadelphia in 1819. This guy, Michel, also drew a large crowd. But he had trouble getting his balloon inflated. The crowd became impatient and rioted. They destroyed Michel's balloon and all his gear and then stole his money.

We packed up in record time that afternoon.

During the third session, I took each member of the ground crew for a walk through the center of the envelope. They loved it. There's nothing like strolling through a huge billowing balloon to make a person

feel insignificant. It's as though you're in the belly of
a big dinosaur. Each time I went through, I inspected
the material for weaknesses and overheating. I also
checked the lines from the rip panel and maneuvering
vent.

It was getting exciting. Friday was only a day away.
The girls thought the practice sessions were fun, but I
saw them as lethal shots of adrenaline. I was getting
pumped higher and higher until I was sure I was going
to explode from the pressure.

Even as busy as we'd become, rehearsing, getting
tanks ready, loading and unloading the gondola and
envelope, the week passed with incredible slowness. I
was so close to finding out the truth that my fingers
had taken on a permanent condition of shaking. I was
stuck in a dream. Everything was becoming less and
less real. I was afraid.

On Thursday night I couldn't sleep at all.

At first I thought it was the flight that was scaring
me. As the girls always pointed out, the last time I'd
gone up, I'd crashed. I soon realized, however, it was
my amnesia that had me worried. Part of me was
anxious to find my family. Another part of me was
afraid I wasn't going to have any kind of a recall at all,
that I wouldn't remember, period.

We'd always been confident the launch was going to
bring my memory back. We'd never doubted it. It had
worried Dr. Essig so much that he'd refused to give me
permission to go. Now I was wondering why we'd all
been so positive. I mean, what reasons did I have to be
so sure?

That's what was really scaring me. There was no
guarantee that I'd be cured. There never had been.

Chapter Ten

On Friday morning I felt as though a bomb had exploded in my stomach. I immediately went outside to check launch conditions. The wind was nonexistent. I called the local FAA flight service station for information on the current weather and the forecasted weather. Cristy and Edon tiptoed from the bedrooms and came to stand behind me as I listened to the report.

"Well?" they whispered after I hung up the receiver.

"The surface winds are at about ten knots."

"So?"

"So it's a perfect day for flying!"

We all scrambled to our bedrooms to dress. We left fifteen minutes later, right on schedule. Trixie and Julie were waiting outside their houses. Every now and

then someone would make a joke and we'd all laugh.
Not because it was so funny, but because we were nervous. Cristy passed out some fruit and doughnuts, and
nobody was able to eat.

The sun was beginning to rise, and the sky was a
muted pink by the time we arrived at the health club.
I briefed them on their responsibilities and duties one
last time before we got started.

We unloaded the basket and canvas bag from the
trailer. The envelope was next. We stretched it out and
attached it to the gondola. I tended to the cables myself and, once again, I checked the fuel lines for leaks.
We set up the fan next, and as the balloon began
breathing to life, I took a walk through it, inspecting
for tangled lines or any other kind of trouble.

I looked over the burner system one last time, made
sure Cristy knew everything she needed to for the
chase and then I ignited the burners.

They were loud, hot and matched the burning I felt
inside me. The long blue flame licked at the air, sending heat outward. Soon the great giant dinosaur rose
from the bed of grass, rounded itself out and lifted the
gondola upright.

The girls shouted and shook each other's hands.

Cristy shut off the fan. I instructed them to keep
their hands on the rim while Julie untied the handling
line from the car.

"I want to come!" Edon said suddenly.

I didn't answer right off, but I pulled the trigger on
the blast valve for a short interval. "Get in then."

"Edon, no!" Cristy tried to hang on to her leg.

"I'm his nurse! I have to!" She climbed over the
rim and clung to a cable dramatically.

I guess I'd really have to do some acting now. I still planned on keeping my recall a secret to protect the doc. If I started behaving strangely, I would have to tell Edon it was just the way I responded to flying.

"Okay, hands off!" Everyone backed away from the basket. I blasted, and slowly the gondola lifted from the ground.

"Good grief!" Cristy gasped. "Be careful!"

"Adiós, au revoir, sayonara!" Edon called in a shaky voice. "Take B.A. out! Don't paint my bedroom!"

"Can I have your gray suede boots?" Julie shouted.

"Please take care!" Cristy waved frantically.

We floated higher and higher until finally we couldn't hear their voices anymore, and they looked like panicked ants running in circles and colliding with one another to get into the car. Edon kept her gaze up instead of down. I knew if she was feeling anything like me, there was a volcano inside her.

"Relax," I told her.

"You relax. I'm going to stay tense for a while."

There was a small pond situated on the rolling lawns behind the health club. It appeared both shallow and deep. Immense and yet tiny.

Hanging in the air altered your perspective on things. A grungy pond was now a shimmering emerald. The lawns had unfolded into velvet blankets. Houses became shoe boxes. Roads were long, ugly zippers.

It was wonderful looking down instead of up all the time, floating, instead of feeling like lead. I made a series of blasts so that our visibility extended for miles and miles, nearly over the entire valley.

"We're so high," Edon said, peeking over the rim.

"Yeah. It's great, isn't it?" I studied the area below us. It was a mixture of desert and farmland, ranches and residential subdivisions. The wind was blowing us gently to the north, toward the mountains.

"I've been over this area before," I announced.

Edon wasn't listening. She was leaning over the rim now, staring.

I couldn't remember exactly when I'd flown this route, but I was beginning to think it was recent. The mesquite trees had been green with leaves then, as they were now. Maybe it had been sometime in early summer.

"Look, Mason! A deer!" Edon pointed to a panicked animal, bounding across the foothills.

I thought of the small herd of deer I'd seen on the trip over the Grand Canyon. The wind shears had nearly done me in. I meditated on what had happened, and the palms of my hands began to sweat. Most of the journey was a blank, yet what I could remember of it gave me unmistakable chills of fear. Especially now, when there were so many visual effects that were reminding me of the flight.

I noticed that a part of me kept wanting me to think of something else, and my uneasiness continued to mount.

I forced myself to stay with my thoughts. I tried to see the Canyon as it had been on that day. So vast and awesome. So beautiful and deadly.

Deadly. The word repeated itself in my mind like a neon light. The trip *had* been deadly. Nobody in his right mind flies the Grand Canyon. It's suicide.

Deadly.

Time seemed too slow.

I knew I was going to have a recall. My stomach was in knots. My head was screaming. I knew I was going to have a recall because I wanted to have a recall.

I could bring it on. I could do it. I could force myself to remember.

I turned away from Edon.

The doc had been right. My amnesia was emotional, not physical. I didn't know why I suddenly knew it. But I did.

I'd been forcing the block in my mind. I was keeping myself from the truth.

I blasted so that our line of flight would stay even. The balloon was making me face it. It was giving me courage to think. Cares shrink when you float in the air. A lot of worries stay on the earth.

What was I so afraid of? Why did I have to go to such extremes to remember? What had happened to me?

I blasted. My eyes blurred with tears. My heart drummed so loudly in my chest that I heard it in my brain.

I knew what the truth was.

I knew why.

There was a stabbing pain in my heart. So much sadness swelled in my chest that I thought I would collapse from the burden of it. Tears fell down my cheeks in thin, warm streams.

I knew what the truth was.

I knew why.

Mason Redford from Moscow had no family.

He didn't have parents.

He didn't have brothers or sisters.

He didn't have anyone.

I wiped the wetness from my eyes. I couldn't see anything.

"Mason!" Edon cried. She half jumped to my side. She started hugging me, trying to calm me down.

Chapter Eleven

My mom and dad are dead, Edon." I felt my heart breaking. "They died in a car accident six months ago."

Edon started to sob. "I'm so sorry, Mason. I'm so sorry..."

I'd stayed home that night. There had been homework to do. I had a test the following day. Mom and Dad had left around six. The dinner party was supposed to start at seven-thirty.

I hadn't thought anything of the sirens at first. We'd often heard them at night. But these sirens had been close by. And there had been so many of them. More and more emergency vehicles had continued to arrive.

I hadn't been able to concentrate on my homework. I'd put on a jacket and gone outside. Deciding the commotion was too far away to walk to, I'd gone back into the house and turned on the stereo to mute the noise.

An hour later there had been a knock on the door. A policeman was standing outside.

"Mr. Reynalds?" he'd said.

"Yes."

The policeman had groped for the words. "I hate to say this, son, but there's been a terrible accident and your parents...your dad and mom...they're dead...."

"That money was mine," I now said to Edon. "Life insurance. I threw my wallet overboard. I was the one who removed the owner's plaque. I wrote the note." I wished I could go back. I wished I could've done what the doc had said and stayed out of the sky. I wished I didn't have a memory. I couldn't stand the sadness. The awful, aching sadness.

"I couldn't take it anymore. I flew over the Grand Canyon to end the loneliness."

"You tried to kill yourself, Mason?"

"The grief was too heavy. I missed Mom and Dad too much." We were losing altitude. I gave a series of short blasts. I tried to collect my thoughts. There were so many now. So much confusion inside me.

"Let's go down, Mason." Edon looked worried, and her complexion had paled. "Let's find Dad. He should know what happened."

"No. Too many problems down there."

"We have to go down, Mason!"

I thought about jumping.

Then I remembered the Grand Canyon again. I didn't want to die. I'd never wanted to die. *I just wanted my parents to live.* With amnesia my parents weren't dead. They weren't alive, but they weren't dead. I wondered why I'd remembered them. What had made me think again.

"You're not alone anymore, Mason."

I looked at Edon's red eyes. "What?"

"You're not alone anymore. Before the crash you were alone, but now you're not. You have us. We're your friends."

A strange sense of relief came over me as though I'd suddenly remembered a forgotten present. My loneliness had been so overwhelming, but now there was something warm inside me. It was a small flame compared to the raging fires of grief. But it was there. And it was more than I'd had before. "Yes, that's right." My voice sounded odd. Too soft. "I know the Essigs now. The doc, and you, and Martha."

Edon nodded and swallowed new tears. "Things will be better. We know how you feel." She glanced up at the envelope. "Please, Mason. Let's go down now."

Cristy had done a good job keeping up with the balloon. She'd chased us and was now parked where the gondola was sinking to the earth. To my surprise, the doc's car was pulling up behind her.

The basket touched the earth with a slight bump. I yanked the rope so that the deflation port opened and the envelope floated to the ground. The big dinosaur fainted into piles of material. Julie, Cristy and Trixie ran to the gondola, all of them talking at once, chattering about the dead ends they'd hit and how much fun it had been chasing us. Cristy asked Edon how she liked flying, but instantly fell silent when she saw our faces.

"I hope you won't be mad about me calling Dad," she ended hesitantly. "I was getting nervous about your landing. I thought it would be safer if he was here." She looked at Edon curiously, and Edon shook her head. We climbed over the rim. I walked over to the doc, who was getting out of his car, yelling. He sensed something was wrong immediately.

I looked into his small dark eyes. "You were right, Doc," I half whispered. "My amnesia. I was doing it myself."

The doc stepped toward me, his expression becoming grim. "You don't have a family, do you, son?" he asked quietly.

"No, sir. My parents are dead. You knew that, didn't you?"

He shrugged. "I was hoping I was wrong. But things kept adding up that way." He rubbed my shoulder. "I'm sorry, Mason. I'm sorry you had to find out this way. I was hoping I could make things easier for you."

I heard myself laugh. It was a tense, high-sounding noise. The doc didn't have a screw loose. I did. He'd shown more sense than any of the rest of us. "My name is Mike Reynalds," I said, feeling as if someone should know.

We packed up the rig, and the doc agreed to drive me to my house. I wanted to see it, although I'm not sure why. There were so many times I'd dreamed about walking up the sidewalk to the porch, ringing the doorbell and waiting for my parents to see me. They'd run out, throw their arms around me and shower me with kisses. I'd never been able to make out their faces. But now, all too painfully, I saw Mom's smile as clear as a bell. And Dad's deep-set eyes. He'd always had wrinkles around his eyes. Happy lines.

You never forget people when they die. You can't, even if you try.

That was why I'd arranged the flight over the Grand Canyon. I'd planned that trip without any intention of coming back. I'd advertised for some helpers and paid for a one-time ground crew. In case they'd gotten curious, I'd told them I was going to contact some people on the other side of the Canyon to help me pick up the rig.

They'd never given it a second thought.

I'd told most of my friends I was taking a cruise to help me relax and get over the accident. I'd been so messed up emotionally that everyone had thought it was a great idea.

The money, with the note, was going to be my message to the world. I'd known it would make the news. A hundred thousand dollars means just about everything to people nowadays. Unless they lose their loved ones. Then they realize it's as important as dust.

The doc stopped in front of my house. It was in a nice neighborhood, like the Essigs'. My father had been the district manager for an insurance company, which is why my parents had so many life policies.

I got out of the car. The doc and Edon followed me up the sidewalk.

Summer weeds had grown in the front yard and along the driveway. Two bushes had died from lack of water.

"This is a nice house, Mason," Edon said, her words coming out awkwardly.

"Thanks. It's mine now, I guess. Dad had mortgage insurance."

Dr. Essig whistled. "Your dad and mom were really looking out for you, Mason. They left you everything you needed."

I reached down and yanked up a weed. "Oh, I don't know. A brother and sister, or an aunt or uncle, would've been nice."

"Don't you have any relatives at all?" Edon asked, ignoring the doc's disapproving gaze.

"Nope. Both sides of the family are only children for two generations back. Not another Reynalds around, as far as I know."

"Well, I'm going to have plenty of kids when I get married. At least three of each," Edon announced firmly.

A red sports car screeched to a stop in front of the house. "Hey! Mike! Is that you?" A tall dark-haired boy hopped out.

It was John Burkes, one of many forgotten buddies.

"Where ya been?" he asked, jogging up the sidewalk. He looked happy to see me. Almost relieved. "We were thinking you'd never get back. You didn't write, you worm! Not even a postcard!"

I didn't offer an excuse. To try to explain everything would've been impossible. I wasn't up to it yet. Instead I introduced the doc and Edon. "So how are things going, John?"

"Oh, you know. The same. I enrolled in ASU."

"That's great, John."

"What are you going to do?"

My throat closed in. "I haven't decided yet."

He kicked at the ground with the toe of his tennis shoe. "I hate to bring this up, but Janie's pretty upset with you. She was expecting to hear at least something. A letter, a postcard. She says even morons know how to punch out a number on the phone." He looked at Edon.

"Yeah. I'll have to give her a call."

The doc must have known how hard it was for me to have the conversation with John. He clapped his hands together and announced that it was time for us to be going. John looked surprised, probably thinking, "Time to be going where?" I shook his hand and told him I'd stop by sometime soon.

"Who's Janie?" Edon asked as we were getting into the car.

"She's just a friend. I've known her since I was a freshman. She moved to our high school from New Jersey somewhere."

Janie. I'd forgotten all about her. A year ago I was sure I loved her. We even talked about marriage after we finished school—in the future sometime. Now I could scarcely remember her face. It seemed like years since we'd talked.

I sure didn't love her anymore.

I wondered how many other things I'd forgotten. How many people, commitments and sections of my life.

I'd had a job at a retail department store. Did I remember to quit before the balloon flight over the Grand Canyon? I was captain of a city league baseball team. Had I told them I was going to be gone for the summer? Or was I missing games every week?

The doc helped me unload the gondola. It reminded me of the many times my dad and I would lug it back into the garage after our journeys. My family had loved ballooning. We used to go up at least once a month, sometimes more.

My eyes blurred again, and I excused myself to go to my room. I felt bad about the doc and all the things I'd thought he was guilty of. He'd told me that if I'd asked Officer Penners if any of the missing person reports involved a balloon flight, he would've said no. Dr. Essig had been much more specific when he'd spoken to the police. That's why he'd been so sure none of the reports were about me.

No one knocked on my door or said anything to me for a long time. I lay on the bed for hours, thinking and remembering, remembering and thinking. Finally I got up and started to pack. There weren't a lot of clothes to take, but there was enough to fill a couple of paper bags. I took the bottled sailboat from the shelf. I knew it was presumptuous, but I was going to ask the doc if I could take it with me. I thought about B.A., too. I liked the mutt. He was going to the bathroom outside as much as he was inside these days. I wanted to take him along for company, but I thought about Melissa and Edon and how badly they'd always wanted a dog. I decided it would be best to leave B.A. here.

I heard the door click open, and Melissa snuck into the room. "Mason?" she said softly.

"What Melissa?"

"I'm sorry about your mommy and daddy. They went where Wayne went, didn't they?"

I closed the drawer. "Yes. I guess so."

"What are you doing?"

"I'm packing."

Her eyes got big and round. "Are you goin' on a trip?"

"I'm going home."

She left, and I thought about how much I was going to miss her. She was a good kid. A very clever girl for five.

A knock sounded on the door, and I said, "Come in." I had finished with my clothes. All I needed now was something to pack them in.

I stood up in surprise as Edon, Cristy, Mrs. Essig, Melissa and the doc marched into the room. Every one of them was frowning.

"What do you think you're doing?" Edon stepped forward.

"I'm packing."

"Why?"

I looked at her. I looked at all of them. "I'm going home. In case you've forgotten, I've been cured."

"Excuse me, but what do you call this place?" she demanded.

"I don't know. I don't understand." They were making me very nervous.

"Well, do you call this place a house, or a home?"

Mrs. Essig joined Edon and held her hand. "What Ed is trying to say, Mason, or Mike, is that a home isn't just a house. A home is where the people you love are. Do you see what we're trying to say?"

I dropped my look from their faces to the floor. *A home is where the people you love are.* "I can't impose on you like this anymore. I haven't been doing very well. I have a lot of problems." My skin burned, and I knew that if I wasn't careful they would see me cry.

Cristy hurried over to the bed and sat beside me. "You know, a very smart guy gave me some very good advice once. He said things won't always stay the way they are. To recover from real sadness takes time."

"That's right, Mason." Edon plopped down on the other side of me. "Some things just take time."

"But it's been nearly a year." I picked up the sailboat.

"Time."

"And I've tried everything."

"Time." They put their arms around my shoulders. "Why don't you ever listen to us, Mason?"

I felt some of the pain blow away, and suddenly I was laughing.

"We'd like to be your relatives now, Mason." The doc came forward. "We need you as much as you need us. Stay here, and we can all be a family." He hesitated, then cleared his throat. "Will you have us, son?"

Was he kidding? I tossed the sailboat over my shoulder and tried to grab as many of the Essigs to me as I could.

Now we had all the time in the world.

First Love from Silhouette

COMING NEXT MONTH

A RISKY BUSINESS
Janice Harrell
When Mary Ann and Adam decide to do a little detective work on the neighbors, they end up finding more than they'd bargained for—and not only about the neighbors.

ALLEY CAT
Lee Wardlaw
Why did Alley Cat, KTUNE's sexy new disk jockey with the sultry voice, turn down all public appearances? Was it just part of her act, or was she at heart a little scaredy-cat?

SOMETHING TO TREASURE
Judi Cross
Had prosaic computer-buff David really seen a mermaid, or had he flipped his disk? Already she had him swimming in circles! Was it too late to reprogram?

THE BOY IN WHITE
Tessa Kay
Why did a gorgeous stranger persist in following Kate all around the beautiful island of Corfu? Was he looking for trouble—or romance?

AVAILABLE THIS MONTH:

CAT'S CRADLE Candice Ransom	**UP IN THE AIR** Carrie Lewis
SPOILED ROTTEN Brenda Cole	**KISS OF THE COBRA** Miriam Morton

NOW YOU CAN GET ALL THE FIRST LOVE BOOKS YOU MISSED.... WHILE QUANTITIES LAST!

To receive these FIRST LOVE books,
complete the order form for
a minimum of two books,
clip out and send together with
check or money order
payable to Silhouette Reader Service
(include 75¢ postage and handling) to:

In the U.S.:
901 Fuhrmann Blvd.
P.O. Box 1397
Buffalo, NY 14240

In Canada:
P.O. Box 609
Fort Erie, Ontario
L2A 5X3

QUANTITY	BOOK #	ISBN #	TITLE	AUTHOR	PRICE
☐	129	06129-3	The Ghost of Gamma Rho	Elaine Harper	$1.95
☐	130	06130-7	Nightshade	Jesse Osborne	1.95
☐	134	06134-X	Killebrew's Daughter	Janice Harrell	1.95
☐	135	06135-8	Bid for Romance	Dorothy Francis	1.95
☐	136	06136-6	The Shadow Knows	Becky Stewart	1.95
☐	137	06137-4	Lover's Lake	Elaine Harper	1.95
☐	138	06138-2	In the Money	Beverly Sommers	1.95
☐	139	06139-0	Breaking Away	Josephine Wunsch	1.95
☐	143	06143-9	Hungarian Rhapsody	Marilyn Youngblood	1.95
☐	144	06144-7	Country Boy	Joyce McGill	1.95
☐	145	06145-5	Janine	Elaine Harper	1.95
☐	146	06146-3	Call Back Yesterday	Doreen Owens Malek	1.95

QUANTITY	BOOK #	ISBN #	TITLE	AUTHOR	PRICE
☐	147	06147-1	Why Me?	Beverly Sommers	$1.95
☐	161	06161-7	A Chance Hero	Ann Gabhart	1.95
☐	166	06166-8	And Miles to Go	Beverly Sommers	1.95
☐	169	06169-2	Orinoco Adventure	Elaine Harper	1.95
☐	171	06171-4	Write On!	Dorothy Francis	1.95
☐	172	06172-2	The New Man	Carrie Lewis	1.95
☐	173	06173-0	Someone Else	Becky Stuart	1.95
☐	174	06174-9	Adrienne and the Blob	Judith Enderle	1.95
☐	175	06175-7	Blackbird Keep	Candice Ransom	1.95
☐	176	06176-5	Daughter of the Moon	Lynn Carlock	1.95
☐	178	06178-1	A Broken Bow	Martha Humphreys	1.95
☐	181	06181-1	Homecoming	Elaine Harper	1.95
☐	182	06182-X	The Perfect 10	Josephine Wunsch	1.95
☐	185	06185-4	Stop Thief!	Francis Dorothy	1.95
☐	187	06187-0	Birds of A Feather	Janice Harrell	1.95
☐	188	06188-9	Tomorrow and Tomorrow	Brenda Cole	1.95
☐	189	06189-7	Ghost Ship	Becky Stuart	1.95

Your Order Total $ _____

☐ (Minimum 2 Book Order)

Add appropriate sales tax $ _____

Postage and Handling   _____.75

I enclose   _____

Name _____

Address _____

City _____

State/Prov. _____ Zip/Postal Code _____

FL-RO2B